MITCHIE

By Catherine Blackfeather

Text copyright © 2013 Catherine Blackfeather

Cover Design by Fae Varriale

All rights Reserved

Chapter 1

Mitchie walked quickly along the street, her oversized boots squelching through the mud and horse-droppings. The basket she carried, hooked on one arm, was almost empty, banging on her hip in time with her steps. She saw some urchins playing on a street corner, throwing dice and scuffling with each other. She felt a brief flare of envy at their freedom. Not like her. She had to work morning, noon and night for Mr Tranche – Reverend Tranche – his only servant. And she got nothing for it, only a roof over her head and food. The clothes she wore were not much better than the urchins' - a worn brown dress and mob-cap pulled down over her hair, framing her face. She'd worn that dress since she was eleven, taking it in all down the side seams and the hem to fit her then, and gradually letting it out over the years since. Now her small breasts were beginning to push against the fabric of the bodice. Thin as she was, she still struggled to fasten the buttons each morning when she dressed at first light. But she hated the thought of asking Mr Tranche to let her get a new dress, seeing his eyes on her breasts, her body, noticing why the old one didn't fit. She didn't want to do anything that would make him think of her in that way. The nights when he didn't come at her in the tiny attic room were the only good thing she had to look forward to. She knew when he'd come. She'd hear the creak of his step on the stair, and she'd put away the picture of her mother and douse her candle, as if lying in the dark would keep her any safer.

When he'd finished and departed back down the creaking stairs, casting one last, hate-filled look at her in the flicker of his candle-flame, before leaving her in the dark again, she would lie for hours without sleep, her whole body and soul a bruise.

And now there was this other thing. After all this time of Mr Tranche coming at her like that, since she was eleven, since her Momma died and he kept her on "Taking her in and providing a home for her out of his goodness" - so they all called it; after she had got used to the pain of it, didn't bleed any more after the first few times- now- blood was coming from - that place. She kept bleeding from that same place he put his thing in, and she knew she was going to die. It'd go away for a while, but then it'd come back again, and she knew it must be because of what he was doing to her, and it had to mean she was going to die like her Momma had, bleeding from there and screaming, covering the whole bed with blood till she went white and quiet, and then never moved again. And they took her away, and the mattress off the bed and burned it. And then they talked about where Mitchie should go, but no-one wanted her, and so they said she had to stay with Mr Tranche, because he was such a good man. And she knew her Momma had died because Mr Tranche came at her, like he came at Mitchie now. He made her bleed like that, and she died. Now Mitchie was going to die too. Mr Tranche was killing her sure as if he strangled her or poisoned her. But no-one cared when he killed her Momma. Who was there to care now about Mitchie?

She had to get to the butcher for Mr Tranche's dinner meat. Tuesday was always liver. If she dawdled she'd be late with all her chores and he'd notice the hearth wasn't as black and shiny as it should be, just like his tall black hat he put on in front of the mirror every day, while she stood holding his coat for him.

She wondered if he came at all those ladies he went to do good for, like he did good for her when he came at her. But somehow Mitchie thought ladies weren't made the same as low-class girls like her. They didn't bleed. She didn't think the ladies she saw in the chapel at the front with their husbands even had bottoms or anything like that. She wasn't sure they even had legs like her, with their large crinoline skirts – they just seemed to glide along. She couldn't imagine them having to let Mr Tranche come at them like that. And in any case- if they did- wouldn't they all be afflicted like her, bleeding and dying?

She found a gap in the mounds of horse dung piled at the sides of the road and cut across to the other side. The boys playing dice were behind her now and she was on a busier street. Wagons and carriages jostled past. Mitchie wove her way through the knots and clumps of people, baskets like the one she carried bumped her. She held her own with both hands in front of her now, so it wouldn't tangle with anyone else. She hated this, people backing into her, stepping in front of her, pushing against her. She would always try to walk the street without touching anyone, or being touched. She didn't know why, it just bothered her, like stepping on the cracks in the paving of the raised side-walks on either side of the main street.

The butcher was down that side street. She'd get that then go for the rest after. She ran over the list; candles, stove-black, mothballs, some carrots and onions to go with the liver..... Seeing a gap open between two carts, she stepped out into the road to cross over. One of the carts was piled high with old clothes, off to the paper-mill, maybe. The cart lurched on a pot-hole- they were bad, even on this street- the heavy rains and ice of winter opening them anew as fast as they filled them in. A bundle of clothes fell off almost on top of Mitchie. Without thinking Mitchie seized them and jumped over the pot-hole, in between two carts coming the other way and was on the other side without a soul noticing her. She ducked down the street with the butchers, but then dodged into an alley she knew went back parallel with the street she had just left, running down the back of the shops and hotels that lined that street.

She looked at what she held. Maybe something she could use for a new dress, or to patch into her old one. Oh no!! There was a pair of men's pants and a thick woollen homespun shirt, way too good to be made into rags for paper. But no use to her. The pants were coarse grey wool, made for a labourer, she couldn't patch that into her brown dress. She held them up to herself. Quite small, a boy's size. They'd been bundled together, handed over to the rag and bone man and placed on the pile in the cart as they were, still folded together.

A thought moved in Mitchie's mind. She'd always wanted to be a boy, who could go anywhere, like the urchins she saw on the streets, doing odd-jobs in the open air, not stuck inside a house, slaving away for a master who came at her in the night. She looked at the clothes again and looked round. Not here! She stood in thought a moment, breath suddenly ragged. Yes! This was it! Her chance! She didn't want to die. Life was out there beckoning to her. Discarding the basket, she ran.

When the Rev Tranche raised the alarm later that day, after he got back from visiting the wealthy and "doing good", a search was made throughout the town. They found the basket where it lay in the narrow alley near the butchers. No-one reported seeing anything, suspicious or otherwise. No-one had noticed Mitchie as she headed away. If anyone had seen a small thirteen year old change from a girl to a boy, hacking off her hair with a penknife and tying strips torn from her dress around the waist of her pants in place of a belt, then they weren't the kind who would report any such thing to those who were searching.

But they found a worn brown dress, torn and soaking two days later in the river and Rev Tranche identified it as the one he had so generously clothed his little charge in. They examined the tears on the dress and decided they had not been made by a bear, as there was no blood. It was concluded that Mitchie had been abducted by person or persons unknown, stripped and goodness knows what else had been done to her, before her body was disposed of so carefully it had not turned up. The town derived great pleasure in discussing – or rather – not discussing, but skirting round the subject with horrified whispers and hands held to hearts, and eyes raised upwards and suitable gasps of horror- what might have been done to "that poor girl" before she met her end in a hidden grave. Eyes would turn to Rev Tranche in sympathy, he being such a good man and after all his kindness to that poor motherless child, only for it to come to this, as if somehow he had been cheated in some way to see all his good work wasted.

Chapter 2

Mitchie survived. She was strong and wiry after years of hard labour with her "benefactor". She knew the meaning of work too, and would set to willingly at any task she could find that paid her in coins or food. She knew it would be dangerous to stay where she was, it was quite a small city and it would only be a matter of time before her real identity came to light. So she made her way Westwards into the new, open lands. Canada was vast and empty, but people were moving into it to settle. Mitchie, being willing and hard-working, would find a way to get a lift from one place to another, or in settled areas she'd just walk. She worked alongside other men and boys. She could wield an axe to split logs as well as any boy. And she was handy round a cook-fire too. The men would josh and talk roughly. They'd tell tales about women, exaggerated tales that embarrassed and fascinated all the young boys. They'd all be ribbed about their virginity, not just Mitchie. They'd even give the youngsters advice like "Make sure you wash it every day or you'll get awful sore and you won't even be able to sit in a saddle" they'd tell them. And they talked about women's "time" when you don't mess with them, how they'd be so gosh-darned ornery you'd have better luck with a she-bear. Gradually Mitchie came to understand that she was not going to die of that mysterious bleeding, but she had to conceal it utterly, because no male ever had such a thing happen to them.

She never stayed long in one place. She kept herself dirty and her hair a matted, chopped mess. She swore and farted and spat with the best and she learned to fight, that is, to take a beating as well as handle her fists herself. There were always men who took more interest in boys than women and they'd find Mitchie attractive with her large dark eyes and fine-boned face. She learnt to spot those men and always took care where she slept, having many years' experience of what they would get up to in the night.

There was a railway built all the way across to

the Pacific Coast, and even though Mitchie could never pay for a ticket, she managed to make use of it to travel. The further West she got, the easier it was to cadge some work around the depots and stations. The country was full of wanderers, from all parts of the world, and there were always odd-jobs a willing boy could take on, while the men got the real well-paid, heavy labouring work. She could help out on the numerous spurs that led off the main line, taking water to the teams of men all working in unison, lifting the heavy iron tracks and hammering them in place. Or helping in the cook tents, though they tended to want her to wash for that, which she never liked to do too often. She liked it in the open air, though it was freezing in winter and there were all manner of bears and coyotes to look out for. The emptiness of the Prairies appealed to her – no crowded cities, no filth, no churches and ministers. But you couldn't live out there, not unless you could farm. And that was a hard life. She used to look at the Indian women standing round the edges of the camps, and wonder what they used to live on before the whites came. The older men would tell tales of great herds of buffalo, but she never saw any of them.

After nearly three years, Mitchie found herself in a small mining town up under the edge of the Rockies. There wasn't much there in the way of real buildings: one big general store that served as a saloon too; a few other buildings, some of them half-built; but many were living in tents and wagons- a common sight in many settlements Mitchie had passed through. She looked around to see where she might get some work and food and saw a largish house a way off up a slight rise on the edge of the settlement. She made her way up to that and found a way round to the back. There was a bit of cleared ground leading back up to the trees, with a lean-to and a woodpile. A fat-looking girl was out by the woodpile, trying to split a log. By the way she was handling the axe she wasn't right sure what she was doing with it. Seeing her chance, Mitchie put down her pack and ambled closer. The girl raised the axe, muttering under her breath. Her face was red and she was puffing little clouds of breath in the cold fall air. She grunted and brought the axe down towards the up-ended log, caught it on the edge and it toppled over.

"That damn McCabe! How come I gotta do this?" Her cheeks wobbled a bit and she wiped her face. Mitchie stepped up behind her.

"You need some help with that, Miss?"

The girl turned. She didn't look much more than two, three years older than Mitchie.

"I can handle a axe real good, Miss, let me do that for you." She stepped forward, holding out her hand. The girl handed the axe to her and backed off.

Putting on her most earnest and well-meaning look, Mitchie said, "Don' worry, Miss, I'll soon have you a pile o' wood," and grinned.

The girl kind of simpered and said, "Sure! Be my guest."

Mitchie set to. She could have lined a road from the East coast to the West with the logs she had split for people. The axe was blunt, so after the first log she went and found a whetstone in her pack and expertly put an edge on. The girl was standing in the doorway, looking at her, her arms folded across her ample bosom. Mitchie grinned and said "There, you won't be so likely to chop your foot off next time, Miss."

She was working it. There was bound to be good eating in a house with such a fat girl. She split a pile big enough to fill the basket nearby and hefted it into the back door.

"Where you want this?" she lugged the awkward load over to the range. The kitchen was none too clean, but the girl poured her a cup of coffee and gave her a slice of cold meat pie. Mitchie grinned.

"Thank you, miss. After I've ate this I'll do you a whole lot more, if you like. Then you won't have to worry 'bout it." She bit into the pie. The girl stood looking at her. The pie wasn't good, but Mitchie'd tasted worse.

"Name's Mitchie," she said, hoping the girl

would do more than just look at her and dimple her cheeks like that.

"Maisie," answered the girl. "How old are you?"

"Ummm. Fifteen, sixteen, I ain't too sure, Miss."

"You ain't that old!! If you were you'd have some whiskers and your voice ain't broke yet."

"I guess," said Mitchie, and left it at that. "You want some more done round here? I work real good."

"Sure."

After Mitchie had split a large quantity of logs, and stacked them tidy under a tarp by the back door, and brought more in, swept up the chippings, carried out a bucket of scraps for the pig out back, climbed a ladder to help Maisie get a pot off a high shelf and hefted a big sack of flour so Maisie could scoop some into a big mixing bowl to start making more of her awful pastry, another woman had come into the kitchen. Even though it was late in the morning by then, her face was puffy with sleep. Her hair was frowzy and fluffy and she wore a housecoat, once brightly coloured, but now faded. Mitchie was just tucking into another slice of the meat pie, thankful her teeth were good enough to bite through the pastry, when she walked in. She sat down on the two-seater sofa by the range and began rolling herself a cigarette. Mitchie stood there awkwardly but Maisie carried on, unconcerned.

"G' mornin' Miss Ellie," she said, continuing to mix flour and lard in the big bowl.

Miss Ellie took a long drag on her roll-up and squinted at Mitchie through the smoke.

"Who's that?" She picked a strand off her lip.

"Oh that's Mitchie, Miss Ellie. He's been helping me round here. Mr McCabe don't seem to be round when I need wood chopping and stuff."

Mitchie nodded to Miss Ellie, putting her pie on the table and dragging the shapeless hat from her head. She nodded and muttered "Miss Ellie," and stood there, the perfect picture of an awkward boy in the presence of an older woman.

"You just get here, Mitchie?" asked Miss Ellie.

"Yes'm, came in today. I could do for you here, Miss. I'm right handy and don't eat much." She looked at the piece of pie with a bite out of it and oozing gravy onto the table top. Miss Ellie shrugged.

"We ain't got nowhere you can stay here, but you're welcome to come and work if you like."

"Oh that's alright, Miss Ellie, I got me a tent and bed-roll. I'm all set up for that. Thank you, Miss Ellie. I'm most thankful to you." She bobbed her head and shuffled her feet, turning the hat in her hands. Miss Ellie took another drag, smiled vaguely at Mitchie and that seemed to be that. Maisie was grinning broadly at her, the dimples really showing in her cheeks. Mitchie grinned back and picked up the pie.

She went and put her tent up round the back of the pigsty. She didn't mind the smell of pig, and it was kind of company. Her tent wouldn't be too easy to spot tucked away like that, and that was the way Mitchie liked it. She'd come in with a group of men who wanted to start mining for themselves, but she didn't want to stay with them if she could get work and food at this house.

She went back and found Maisie in the yard, sitting on a big log and smoking. She smiled at Mitchie and offered her a drag when she sat down next to her. Her dimples were cute. She had dark eyes with a bit of a cast in one, so she seemed to be looking in two places at once, and really fair, freckly skin. She didn't talk, just smiled, so Mitchie said

"I'm right glad to be working here, Miss Maisie. That was real kind of you to speak up for me like that."

Maisie giggled. "You don't have to call me Miss. I'm just Maisie." Smile.

"So... what kind of a establishment is this Mi um..Maisie?"

"Oh, it's a whorehouse. Finest one in a hunerd miles, so they say."

Mitchie looked at Maisie in surprise.

"Are you a whore?"

"Me? Naaah. Not now anyways. Miss Ellie said I din't have to do it no more, now."

Mitchie looked at her, slightly awed. "You done it before though?"

Maisie nodded. "Yeah I done it since I was, oh - thirteen, but I din't really like it, you know. It's better since Miss Ellie come, more high-class like, so's I *could* make more money on it now, I suppose, but Miss Ellie said I was to work in the kitchen and the other ladies'd take care of that side o' business."

In her travels Mitchie had learnt there were ladies who got paid for doing what she'd had done to her by Mr Tranche. She guessed it was as good a living as any, but even now she knew it wasn't going it kill her, she didn't feel tempted to try it. She liked being outdoors.

"I wouldn't want to do that myself," she said out loud. Maisie giggled.

"Well you couldn't do it anyway, you're a boy. Not unless... well, we don't do for that kind of gentleman."

In all her years since fleeing Mr Tranche, Mitchie had never made a slip like that. She took the cigarette from Maisie and dragged on it, casting her a side-long look.

Maisie was not exactly well-endowed with intelligence and Mitchie had fooled even Miss Ellie, who was a much sharper and more experienced person, so her slip wasn't noticed. Maisie continued to sit and say nothing. They finished the cigarette. The birds were singing. A bell started to ring from the other side of the valley, a single repeated clang. Maisie looked up.

"That'll be them Presbyterians. They set up over there. Coming here and spoiling everything, Miss Ellie says."

Mitchie looked across to where the sound came from and saw, small against the backdrop of trees, an unpainted wood building, so new you could almost see the sap oozing from the planks it was made of. It had a small bell turret on top. She decided she and Miss

Ellie were going it get on fine, as their opinions agreed in this importance topic. Mr Tranche had been a Presbyterian.

Maisie stirred on the log.

"The ladies'll all be getting up soon. You want to come and help me clean up inside?" she asked.

"I guess so."

They went into a large room in the front of the building that looked like a saloon, but with soft chairs and chesterfields for everyone to sit on, and small tables in front of them. There was a staircase leading up to a gallery that ran the length of the room, above where the two girls had come in from the kitchen. There were doors along that gallery, leading to rooms that were above the kitchen. The room looked so grand to Mitchie's eyes. The curtains and chairs were in red velvet, and there was a fancy carpet on the floor. There were proper spittoons along the walls, so no-one would spit on the carpet, and there was a fine bar along one wall with a mirror and all. A chandelier was hanging down and there was even a piano. None of the places she had passed through on her way here had looked anything like this, and Mr Tranche's house had been dark and oppressive, though its furnishings had probably been more expensive. To Mitchie's untutored gaze, the front room looked like a palace.

Maisie wandered into the middle of the room, oblivious to Mitchie's reaction. She started to wipe a cloth over the tables, without achieving much.

"See them spittoons? You better empty them. You can do it out back and rinse 'em under the pump."

"Yes'm," said Mitchie. Maisie giggled.

Other women began to appear, all as tousled and frowzy with sleep as Miss Ellie. A man came down too. This was McCabe. Mitchie wasn't sure who he was in the scheme of things, but she just kept on sweeping the floor and polishing things while they all trooped to the kitchen. Maisie said

"You better keep on here. I gotta go make

breakfast for the ladies."

So Mitchie carried on working while the smell of frying bacon filled the room. Some of the women came back and sat chatting with their bacon and bread and coffee, glancing at Mitchie, but dismissing her when they realized she was not a paying customer. McCabe came back in and started cleaning up the bar. He called Mitchie over and set her to washing glasses and wiping down the counter while he emptied the till and began counting money. Miss Ellie sat down with him and began making entries in a large book. The doors to the outside were opened to let in some air and the women drifted back upstairs to their rooms. Mitchie made her way back to the kitchen and sat outside on the big log. Maisie came and sat down beside her. Her plump thigh pressed against Mitchie's as she fitted herself onto the flat part of the log.

"You know, you kinda smell, Mitchie," said Maisie. "When you last take a bath?"

"I dunno. The wagon we was in turned over in

the river a week or two back. I had to swim some, I reckon that'll do me for this year anyway." She grinned at Maisie.

"Awww! You!" Maisie chuckled. "Well, we got a bathhouse here. A real fine one, indoors too. They make the gentlemen clean up some before they go up with the ladies. You could use that."

"Oh no! I couldn't do that!"

"Why not? McCabe's getting it hot now. There's a fancy copper tank for the hot water. You won't find anything finer this side o' the Rockies."

"Well, I'm kind of bashful," stammered Mitchie. "I'll wash up out back later."

Maisie gave her a look.

"You think you got anything I ain't already seen?"

"No, but....."

Maisie tutted. "You can use my room if you like. I got a room all of my own," she said.

"No! Really. I'll be alright. I'll do it later."

Maisie put on a prissy sing-song voice like she was repeating something she'd heard.

"I do declare, young boys are allergic to hot water and soap!"

Mitchie laughed and Maisie's dimples reappeared.

"Here! I found some more t'bacco. You should look out fer stuff when you clean, you missed this. Down the back of the chesterfields is best place to look- you find all sorts, money and all." They rolled up and smoked another cigarette between them.

"It won't get busy till night. Most men are working now," said Maisie in a conversational tone. "You should hear Miss Beryl play that piano, she coulda been famous for it."

"Did she give it up to be a whore?" asked Mitchie.

"Yeah, I guess so."

"Did you give up something to be a whore?"

"No. I just done it coz I figured it'd be better to get paid for it, you know..." she shrugged.

It was a point of view, Mitchie thought.

"So how come you din't like it?"

"Aww well, McCabe brought us here, me and Flossy and Roxanne, and it was just in tents, no better'n that one you got back there... no offence. It was just two bucks a trick and they was lining up outside. McCabe took most of it himself, we weren't making hardly worth a damn. Now, Miss Ellie, she got a high-class place. They pays real money for the ladies here. She went into business with McCabe, but she's the real brains round here. He ain't worth spit." she glanced back at the house. "'Sides, I don't really like 'em - I'd rather..." she tailed off.

"So, that's who McCabe is," thought Mitchie to herself. Out loud she said

"So, you just looks after 'em? The ladies and all? Cooking and stuff."

"Yep! That's me!" Maisie smiled proudly. "Cook and housekeeper. Miss Ellie pays me a proper wage and all."

They sat in silence, smoking and gazing out

across the valley. The smoke of cook fires, clang and bang of tools and the reek of shit and other human smells rose up from the lower ground. There was building work and mining all taking place in a haphazard way below them. They heard men shouting suddenly and a deep cracking sound followed by loud rustling and tearing. A tree fell on the hillside above. The air was moist and cool, the leaves on some of the trees were yellow and orange, though most were spruce and fir. Mitchie knew it would get cold in these parts in winter. She needed a place indoors.

As if in some way tracking her thoughts, Maisie said,

"The hog'll go soon, Skinner'll come up to stick her now it's Fall." She smacked her lips, thinking of the meat they'd get.

"You like black pudding?" she asked.

"Sure. You make that yourself?" Mitchie tried not to look sceptical.

"Naa! Skinner does. Best I ever had. He does the bacon and ham too. Mmmmm!" she wriggled on the log seat. Mitchie rubbed her belly and went "Mmmmm" too. She could see Maisie's eyes linger on her as they laughed. She made a decision.

"I can cook some too, if you want some help in the kitchen."

Maybe it was a mistake, but she was tired of men and their ways. Maybe being in a house full of women would be better. Something about the way Maisie's plump thigh jostled up to her on the log seat felt good to Mitchie.

"Sure! You can help me if you like." A little smile. "You got to clean up some first, though." Mitchie nodded. Cooks always said that.

"Come on then!" Maisie heaved herself off the log, which rocked as her weight left it, making Mitchie catch herself so as not to fall over. They went into the kitchen again and Maisie took a rag and lifted a large kettle off the stove. She carried it across to a door on the other side of the kitchen that Mitchie had taken for a storeroom.

"Open that, will ya," panted Maisie.

Inside was an unmade bed with a packing crate by it as a table, a chair with clothes piled and draped on it, a washstand with a small mirror over it on the wall. There was no window, just a moon-shape cut-out in the door, like it was a privy. Maisie poured the water.

"Here y'are." she went to the chair and fished around and pulled a towel out. She handed it to Mitchie, who stood there, hesitating.

"Alright, so no peeking then!" Maisie laughed and left, sashaying her hips a little as she went.

There wasn't that much hot water, but Mitchie found a jug of cold water already on the washstand, so she mixed that in.

"Nothing for it, then," she thought, and stripped off. She began to rinse herself off. She had indeed allowed herself to get a little overripe. The last gang of men she'd come with had all been uninterested in any kind of personal hygiene, and suspicious amounts of washing would only draw attention. She'd only been able to attend to the rudiments to make sure nothing showed of her monthlies.

She had managed to get all of herself clean, including, finally, her hair, which was the filthiest of all – so filthy even lice tended to shun it – and was using Maisie's brush and comb to try and get whatever knots she could out of it, when the door opened and Maisie walked in with some clean clothes in her hand. The light from the kitchen fell full on Mitchie's naked body, and Maisie stood stock still in astonishment. Skinny as she was with tiny breasts, there was no mistaking Mitchie's gender.

Maisie walked fully into the room and shut the door behind her, eyes on Mitchie's body. Mitchie watched her, trying to gauge her reaction. Maisie's mouth quirked up.

"You're a girl?"

"Please don't let on to no-one!"

Maisie's mouth quirked up a bit more.

"Sure! I won't tell." She held out the clothes, "I brung you these." Mitchie took them and Maisie went over by her bed and lit the lamp on the crate by it. She turned back to Mitchie, who just stood there holding the clothes. Maisie smiled at Mitchie.

"You wanna fool around?" she asked.

"What do you mean?" said a bewildered Mitchie.

"You know...." Maisie began to unbutton her blouse, looking at Mitchie with a broad smile. She opened her blouse and unlaced her bodice, exposing her breasts. Mitchie's eyes went wide with amazement, her mouth had gone dry. Maisie cupped her breasts in her pudgy hands and moved towards Mitchie.

"Come on! Feel them." She wiggled forward and shadows played on her breasts. Mitchie dropped the bundle of clothes and stepped towards Maisie. Her own nipples were standing erect and her hands reached and took a breast in each hand. They were so soft. Her eyes flicked to Maisie's face and back to what she was holding in her hands, her mouth hanging open. Maisie's nipples were standing up too, big and pink. Mitchie put her fingers round them and gently squeezed, she pressed the soft, mounded flesh, excited by the feel and sight of them. Maisie made a small, satisfied chirrup in her throat and her smile widened. She began to unfasten her skirt and under drawers while Mitchie continued to hold and knead her breasts, her breath coming in short through her still-open mouth, till Maisie had to bend over to pull the skirt over her large hips. She went and lay on the bed, naked now. The glow from the lamp cast shadows across her white skin and the downy billows of her belly and breasts and thighs.

"Come on!" She wriggled on the bed, spreading her thighs.

Mitchie had no idea what Maisie wanted of her, but she just climbed on top of Maisie, along the length of her, her own thin body sliding across the soft mounds of belly. She touched her lips to Maisie's, tentatively, but Maisie grabbed her head in both hands and glued her lips to Mitchie's, moving her mouth on Mitchie's, sucking and munching and Mitchie just did the same back. When she felt Maisie's tongue wet in her mouth, she played with it with her own.

Her hands were back on Maisie's breasts, taking on a life of their own, squeezing them and pinching her nipples. They were lovely. She stopped kissing to draw breath a moment and Maisie pushed her head down to her breasts. Mitchie buried her face in them, between them, they flowed around her and felt lovely. She took one nipple in her mouth and sucked. Maisie made that noise again in her throat and wiggled, holding Mitchie's head with one hand while the other went down between her thighs. Mitchie was getting the hang of this now, and she sucked some more at Maisie's nipple while her hands explored the rest of her. She felt like a soft rubber ball, everything Mitchie pressed and squeezed gave then sprung back to shape after. Mitchie felt engulfed in sensation. Maisie was holding her round her ass now, squeezing and kneading her hard buttocks and grinding herself into Mitchie's groin. Mitchie felt a spurt of sensation between her legs, a hot, spreading urgency. She pumped and ground back at Maisie, pushing her leg into a hot, wet place where

Maisie's legs spread apart. They were kissing again, pushing mouth to mouth hard as their groins pushed into each other. Maisie wrapped one leg around Mitchie's and started to make little grunts and whimpers. Faster and faster she pumped herself against Mitchie's leg. She was so wet and warm where she was rubbing herself, Mitchie felt herself all wet too. She didn't know you could feel so good in that place, but it did feel good. They stopped kissing to concentrate on that same place on each other's bodies. Ripples of pleasure gathered and flowed in Mitchie's crotch, she kept working away at it, whenever it faded she found it again and built it back. Maisie's mouth was open and her tongue was flicking out and round her lips, all pink and cute-looking. Her eyes were unfocussed, the squint really pronounced as she grunted and panted under Mitchie.

Suddenly she gave a real loud gasp, like a whimpering groan and her whole body tensed and rose up under Mitchie. She was gripping Mitchie's thigh so hard between her own it almost stopped the blood in Mitchie's leg. Her fingers dug hard into Mitchie's ass, then she fell back, panting, made a couple more thrusts, squeezing Mitchie's leg again between her thighs and finally subsided, making that little groaning chirrup again in her throat. She focussed on Mitchie's face and smiled. Mitchie smiled back. She had no real idea what was going on, but she loved the feel of Maisie's body under hers, and she wanted this, wanted more of it. A doorway opened somewhere inside her. She was surely going to stay here.

The two girls lay side by side, Maisie plumb on her back and Mitchie on her side, gently stroking Maisie's body and gazing at her. She loved the softness and curves of her. She'd had almost nothing to do with any women all her life, after her mother died, and she'd never seen one naked before. In her mind's eye she saw her own thin, wiry body as almost the same as a man's, except with no cock. It was a revelation to her to see and feel all this luscious curviness. Her lips touched Maisie's shoulder, her face, her lips.

Then Miss Ellie called from the kitchen, "Maisie! Where are you? Your pies are ready. You better get out here and take 'em out!"

"Yes Miss Ellie, I'll be right there!" Maisie called back, but made no move to get up. She grinned at Mitchie and kissed her hard. Miss Ellie was quite used to Maisie's slow ways and left the kitchen with a shrug to go and start dressing for the evening's work.

The girls lay and kissed and began to work each other up again. The throb between Mitchie's legs was unfamiliar and delightful. But then an unmistakeable smell of burning wafted from the kitchen. Mitchie said

"I guess you better go see to that."

"I guess so," Maisie sighed grumpily. She sat up, her legs straight on the bed and her belly hanging forward. Mitchie sat up beside her. Their hands still lingered on each other, but Maisie swung her legs over the side of the bed and dragged her drawers over and began to work them up her legs. She stood up to yank them up over her backside while Mitchie gazed, entranced at that rounded mass of female flesh. Maisie glanced back and saw her expression, gave her a flirty look and carried on dragging her clothes on, watching Mitchie watching her, enjoying her rapt attention, deeply flattered by the wide-eyed appreciation she was getting.

"You better get up too."

"Yes'm." Mitchie got up too.

"Don't put them smelly old things back on, I brung you new stuff."

Maisie exited to rescue the pies, while Mitchie put on the clean woollen undershirt, shirt and pants in an assortment of sizes left by various customers. There was even a couple of pairs of socks. The ones Mitchie had were more patches than sock. Maybe she'd get herself a new pair of boots while she was here. She extracted a leather belt from the pile of filthy clothes on the floor and fastened it round her waist, arranged the pants to her liking, hitched up over the belt, and put on the shapeless jacket that concealed everything. She had to wear that, smelly or not. She could take the chance to wash the other stuff later. Winter was coming and she couldn't have too many layers of clothes. She checked herself in the tiny mirror over the washstand. Her hair was pretty ruffled up after all she'd been doing while it was still wet, but she ruffled it further. She'd need to cut that sometime. Maybe Maisie'd do it for her.

She looked back at the bed and suddenly felt unreal. What had just happened? She went to douse the lamp and picked up the pillow from the bed, held it to her and smelled it. It smelt of Maisie, that special cosy bed-smell of a human body, a female body. She felt her lips. She didn't know you could kiss like that, all hot and soft and....tasty. She recalled, with a shudder, Mr Tranche's hard, whiskery lips on hers. But her mouth had stayed shut then, her lips pulled inside, and squirming her face away from his panting and grunting on top of her. That place down below where he used to put his thing so painfully, now felt soft and alive, expectant.

A shy, incredulous grin appeared around her mouth and she replaced the pillow. She peaked out the door to see if the coast was clear and let herself into the kitchen. Maisie's pies looked awful, though one was not really badly burned. She was hacking away at the charred areas, cutting them off, looking quite unconcerned. She gave Mitchie a wide smile and said,

"Have some coffee if you like. I get busy now. I gotta give the ladies their dinner so they can work through tonight." There was a large cabbage and a pile of potatoes on the table.

"Want me to peel them potatoes?"

"Sure, if you want to."

She showed Mitchie the basin to wash them and gave her a small knife. Mitchie dumped the smelly clothes by the back door and set to. Sitting down on a stool with the basin on the floor, peeling the potatoes onto some newspaper, she was on a level with Maisie's ample backside. She couldn't stop herself looking over at it. Thinking about round the front of it. The way she'd pressed and rubbed herself against Mitchie's leg, put her hand down there, her fingers vanishing between her thighs. Mitchie just wanted to put everything down and grab Maisie's ass, feel inside her cleft – she made herself look away and shut her mouth. Maisie smiled to herself, well aware of Mitchie's open-mouthed appraisal of her.

Mitchie gave the potatoes to Maisie who chopped them haphazardly and dropped them into a pot of boiling water. She dug the knife into the cabbage and levered it apart, and chopped up the whole thing, stem and all, and scraped it off the board into another pot. Even in her enamoured state Mitchie couldn't help noticing Maisie seemed to know very little about cooking.

She sipped a coffee then took the peelings to the pig out back, dumping her clothes off at her tent and setting things to rights inside before it got too dark to see. When she got back to the kitchen Maisie was serving up the food to the women. Most of them were already dressed for work. There were six of them, seven including Miss Ellie, and Mr McCabe too. Mitchie stood shyly by the door taking in the sight.

Women she'd met before, in the chapel with Mr Tranche, or on city streets or farmhouses, never wore anything but brown or grey or black or maybe a light beige. She'd never seen dresses in red or purple or green, made of satin and velvet, with ruffles and bows and low-cut necks that showed the tops of their breasts. O my! The women, noticing the bashful boy's entranced gaze were amused.

"Hey Mitchie! Come on over here if you want a closer look!"

Mitchie blushed and took her plate out the back door, to the laughter of the women.

"Don't come in your pants!" one of them called after her.

Maisie was not pleased. She clattered the pans and dishes loudly in the sink, but, since she was so clumsy anyway, no-one noticed.

After the women had eaten all they could bear of Maisie's awful cooking, they moved into the saloon. Mitchie went back in the kitchen to help Maisie and the sound of the piano being played rather well by Miss Beryl, wafted through.

Curious, Mitchie went to look through the doorway that led through to the saloon. There was a step up into that part and Mitchie sat on it and gazed out at the scene. Miss Ellie looked splendid in a dark red satin gown, a kind of feather thing was sticking out of her hair, and a band of pearls on red velvet was tied round her neck, and she had a fan and gloves and all. She'd done something to her face too, painted it, but it looked good, not like Mitchie had always imagined painted Jezebels looked when she'd heard talk of them long ago in chapel. Maisie pushed up next to her.

"It all looks like … like a fairy palace in there with all them silver candles and the chandelier," breathed Mitchie. "I ain't never seen anything so pretty. And Miss Ellie! She looks like a princess all done up like that!"

Maisie's mouth pulled down into a line.

"I guess you like 'em a lot better'n me." It was a statement, not a question. Mitchie looked round at her, surprised.

"Why, Maisie, I'd surely love to see you in a

pretty dress like that. You'd look better'n any of 'em."

"Yeh?" Now it was a question. Maisie attempted a pout, but she was too pleased to do it convincingly.

"Well, if I was wearing one of them dresses it'd be coz I was working the gentlemen, then maybe you wouldn't like that....." she paused, waiting to see what effect that would have on Mitchie. This was all new to her. She'd asked more than one of the women here if they wanted to fool around with her. They would just roll their eyes and say, "No, Maisie, I do not want to fool around with you." They all knew her tendencies. Where their tolerance wore thin was in having to eat her dreadful cooking every day, but Miss Ellie thought it would be bad for business to turn her out. She'd only go back to selling herself in a tent like she was before, and that would undercut the demand for what she was offering. Maisie never took it bad when they turned her down, just lived in a kind of vague hope that one day she'd get lucky. She had once, when she was back in

Mudville, and an older woman, too old to work really, had shown her things, done things with her, in between pimping her to men. Maisie liked that a whole lot better than doing it with men. They were just business. She'd lay back, open her legs and let them get on with it. She'd wash them before and herself after, then wait for the next one.

But now, here was Mitchie, and it was her first time, and Maisie was already looking forward to having more fun with her. She was hers. She didn't want her looking at other women.

Mitchie looked at her earnestly.

"One day I'm gonna buy you a pretty dress like that, and you can wear it every day and look like a princess all the time, and not have to whore or nothing."

"Awwwww! Mitchie!" Maisie grinned, a little overwhelmed by Mitchie's intensity. "Well, come on then, I got something I want to show you."

They left the doorway and went back to Maisie's bed. When they had stripped, Maisie told Mitchie to lie back on the bed.

"You just gotta lie there, let me show you. I'm gonna do yum-yum on you."

She hunkered herself down onto the floor and parted Mitchie's legs. Mitchie looked at her in amazement.

"What're you doing?"

Maisie brought her mouth into the soft fuzz of Mitchie's private place.

"You can't do that! It ….it's dirty!" exclaimed Mitchie.

Maisie started to kiss and lick at Mitchie's cleft. Her fat fingers pulled Mitchie open and her tongue found its way into the pink sweet place.

"Oh, my!" Mitchie's eyes widened. She watched what Maisie was doing with her nose buried right into Mitchie's mound. After a while she had to lean her head back, panting. A flood of intense sensation flowed from Maisie's tongue. She'd never felt anything like it. Boys played with themselves all the time round her in the life she'd been living, but she had never touched herself there. She began to gasp and hold her breath in little gulps as the feeling mounted. Maisie was squeezing her ass while her tongue worked on her, her thumbs parted her ass cheeks and pressed and poked at her, finding yet more sensitive places to play with.

"O my goodness!!" Mitchie pushed herself against Maisie's face. She rose to a climax but Maisie did not stop. The feeling grew and grew, Mitchie thought she was going to burst, everything was focussed on that one point that Maisie gobbled at and licked faster and harder. She was making little grunting noises and Mitchie couldn't stop herself groaning out loud too, but there was so much noise from the piano and the chatter next door, no-one else heard. She came all in a burst that rolled on and on. Oh never stop! I want this forever! Maisie still rubbed and thrust at Mitchie with tongue and fingers, a further burst of bliss opened out in Mitchie's pussy, spreading to her belly and ass and finally she subsided with one last groan. She felt shaken to the roots of her being by that amazing sensation. Maisie got up from the floor and lay half on top Mitchie, who wrapped her legs around her and kissed her, grinding her mouth against Maisie's and still pushing her pelvis at her. She pulled Maisie right onto her, clinging desperately, full of passion and need, wanting Maisie in her, on her, forever.

They fell asleep, squeezed together in Maisie's bed. Maisie would have liked a bit more fun with Mitchie, but Mitchie was almost overwhelmed by the day's events, and lulled by the music next door, she drifted off. Well, Maisie was aiming to have plenty more of that. She thought Mitchie would stay. She wanted her to, didn't never want her to go from her.

In her slow, placid, not very bright way, Maisie believed there was someone special out there for everyone, even someone like her. Mitchie was there now, and it felt like she was what Maisie had always been waiting for, like she already knew her before she met her. She fitted right and that was how it had always been meant to be.

"Mmmm... yum-yum-yum," she whispered to herself, tasting her lips that tasted of Mitchie. She played with herself for a bit, just to finish herself off, but knew it would be more fun when she could get Mitchie to do it to her.

Chapter 3

Mitchie was used to sleeping and waking with the sun, so she woke up long before anyone else in the house. She lay there listening to Maisie snore. She moved her hands lightly over her belly, up to her breast, warm with sleep. She lifted the blanket to look at Maisie's body. The light was dim, but she could see the white of her gleaming in shadowed sleep. She ran her fingers across Maisie's nipple, her aureoles were the lightest pink, not like Mitchie's own dark brown ones. Maisie snored on till Mitchie pinched her nipple to feel it stand up, then Maisie murmured and muttered in her sleep, and turned over, away from Mitchie. She farted and settled back to sleep.

Mitchie drowsed against her back, her hand lying on the swell of her hip. She thought about what Maisie had done with her, that thing with her tongue. "*I never knew anyone could do that!*" she thought. Her curiosity about Maisie's body grew, about that part. She wanted to put her finger there, find out how it felt, she felt herself throb just a bit, thinking about it. She moved her hand further over Maisie's hip and brushed the fuzz of hair below her belly, then let one finger drift to the crack below. Maisie grunted, but didn't waken. She was a real sound sleeper! After another hour Mitchie got herself up and dressed and went to the privy. She took the tobacco from Maisie's [Mitchie's] pocket and went out and sat on the stoop and smoked. Then she went into her own tent. She meant to get the dirty clothes out and start washing them, but somehow found herself laying back on the bed-mat and pulling off her pants. She had a small mirror in her stuff and she got that out and held it down there, so she could see her own privates with it. She spread her legs, looking at the dark little fold, with its fuzz of beard. It was kind of ugly really, little wrinkled thing, but she felt that new sensation begin down there as she looked at it. She pulled the sides of it open and looked at the pinkness within. She ran her two main fingers over it, exploring, delving inwards, rubbing along the length of her slit, feeling it wasn't as wet and slippery as she expected, but then it seemed to become more so, watching herself all the time in the awkwardly held mirror. She found a place that reacted more, a little bump kind of thing. She thought that was where Maisie's tongue had been at last night. She rubbed this, gently at first, then abandoning the mirror, she set to in earnest. Oh yeah! This was it! Why had she never found this out before? All the men did it, when she was out working in the railway camps and farms, there'd always be one of them breathing heavily with his hand moving fast under his blanket, but she didn't have a cock, and she never knew there was something like this that she could do too. Maisie'd showed her.

But now she began to feel sore, it wasn't the same without Maisie, she couldn't get that real good feeling. She pulled her pants back up and got out of the tent, horny and unsatisfied. She went back up to the house and let herself back in Maisie's room, stripped and got back into bed with her. She was sleeping on her back again, snoring. Mitchie put her hand down into Maisie's crack again, not tentative this time, she delved into the moist place and began to rub her. She reached with her mouth and took a nipple in and sucked hard. Maisie's breathing changed. She grunted and opened her eyes. She sighed and wriggled under Mitchie's hand, surfacing further into consciousness. She smiled and cupped Mitchie's head in her hand. Mitchie kissed her, her hand still working on her pussy.

"Hey Maisie! You awake?"

Maisie nodded, her lips still on Mitchie's. "Mmhhm!"

"Can I try that yum-yum thing on you? I want to do it to you, can I?"

This was the nicest wake-up Maisie'd ever had. She made a little whimpering sigh and said,

"You sure can, sweetie, go ahead," and pulled her knees up and apart. Pushing the blanket right off, Mitchie climbed around on the bed and got herself between Maisie's legs. There it was, all folded and wrinkled, like Mitchie's, but lighter, her fuzz a kind of peachy colour. Mitchie sunk between Maisie's fat thighs and tasted that peach. She parted the skin with her fingers and plunged in, her tongue seeking and exploring. Mmmmm, what a taste! What a smell! Indescribable and delicious! She found that little bump thing with her tongue and started to lick and lick at it, pressing her tongue into it as hard as she could. Then licking all round and down into the hot hole there, pushing her tongue in. The taste was stronger there. She lapped at that small, dark well then went back up to the bump again, and Maisie responded, pushing herself into Mitchie's face.

Maisie was panting now and making those whimpering, grunting sounds. Mitchie's own pussy was throbbing in sympathy with the pulses she was feeling from Maisie. Harder and faster she worked, feeling her jaws ache round the root of her tongue at this unaccustomed labour, but she wasn't stopping for nothing. This was the best toffee apple she'd ever licked, and it tasted better every second. Maisie was kind of thrashing round now, her soft, enormous thighs enveloping Mitchie's head. She could hardly breathe she was sunk so deep in Maisie's flesh, her own ass was bobbing up and down. She could feel Maisie's excitement, she pushed and gobbled at Maisie, driving onwards, sensing the climax approach and pushing harder and harder, till something seemed to break, almost, and Maisie made a loud whining groan that went higher and higher. Mitchie's whole face was wet from her nose to her chin and still she kept on, till a flood of delicious juice came out of Maisie's pussy and she heaved herself up, her ass rising from the bed, and her thighs quivering against Mitchie's ears.

Mitchie slowed down. Her tongue was really aching, this was hard work, but oh! So worth it! Maisie subsided into little chirruping whimpers and gasps and held Mitchie's head in place. She tensed and held herself, then released, still holding Mitchie where she wanted her, repeated that a couple more times, while Mitchie still worked her tongue on her, then finally she relaxed and pulled Mitchie up out of her sweating groin, to lie on top of her and filled her mouth with the taste of herself from Mitchie's lips.

Mitchie had come a bit herself along with Maisie, and lay there, replete with sensation, fulfilled for a while at least.

"Mmmmm!" Maisie wriggled her legs and bottom under Mitchie, clenching Mitchie's thigh between her own, "Yum-yum-yum!"

"Yum-yum-yum!" Mitchie echoed. They giggled at each other.

They lay a while, stroking each other and nibbling blissfully at each other's faces and lips. Mitchie's hand travelled across the expanse of Maisie's belly, found her navel. Her finger rested in the soft folds, her eyes in dreamy soft-focus made landscapes of her.

"Mmmmm... you sure are fat, aren't you?" she said appreciatively.

"Yep, always have been. Don't matter, even

when I didn't get much food, I never went skinny like you."

Mitchie looked down at her own tiny-breasted, ribby torso.

"Yeah, ain't nuthin to me really, I guess."

"I ain't complaining none."

Maisie farted. Quite unselfconsciously, she said,

"I gotta go to the privy." She hauled herself up and hunted round for her clothes.

"I guess we better get to work, eh?" said Mitchie.

"Mmm, I guess."

Sitting up behind Maisie, Mitchie wrapped her arms round Maisie's curves, pressing into her back and kissing her shoulder.

"I don't never want to stop fooling with you, Maisie. I want to do this for ever and ever."

Maisie giggled. "Me too, sweetie."

A thought occurred to Mitchie.

"Maisie?"

"Mmhhm?"

"Are we in love?"

This was a whole new concept to Maisie. She thought for a moment, then

"Yeah...yeah! We are!" she turned and held Mitchie's face for a moment, and smiled at her. And then turned back and said "Honey, could you hand my drawers to me?"

Mitchie decided she was going to help Maisie get dressed, with lots of giggling and distractions from the actual process of dressing. But eventually Maisie said

"I need to go real bad, you gotta let me go!" and giggled her way out of the room.

Mitchie dressed slowly, a half-smile on her face. Being in love! That was something everyone talked about, aspired to; eventually it happened to everyone, from what Mitchie had heard in songs and stories, but she'd not seen much evidence of it amongst the men she'd been living around these past three years. Now it had happened to her! She'd never had any ambitions of any sort beyond staying alive, but now! That was not an idle promise she'd made the evening before about getting a dress for Maisie. She felt a plan of sorts – a future-open for her, hazy in the details, but the first idea that her life might amount to anything more than day-to-day survival.

She finished dressing and went out into the kitchen – and stopped dead. Miss Ellie was already there, sitting by the range smoking and sipping coffee. She looked at Mitchie in astonishment, but Mitchie's face was a picture of guilt and embarrassment. She touched her forehead and mumbled "Mornin' Miss Ellie," and almost ran out into the yard.

"Well, well," Miss Ellie thought, "I guess Maisie must have decided to make do with boys after all. I guess that young is as close to a girl as she'll ever get."

Maisie stumped back in to the kitchen holding an apron full of eggs, which she managed not to break when she deposited them on the table. Miss Ellie studied her as she went to make the porridge.

"You fucking Mitchie?" she asked.

Maisie didn't answer, just dolloped a large cupful of oatmeal into the pot.

"Don't put so much in, Maisie dear, you make it too thick. We want to eat it with a spoon not a knife and fork." Maisie grunted and took a small amount back out, but still did not answer Miss Ellie's question.

"Only he just came out of your room, Maisie, and looked fit to die of embarrassment that I saw him."

Maisie poured water into the oatmeal and stirred, still not answering.

"It's no matter to me, only I never thought you'd go with a man if you didn't have to, is all, even if he is only a bitty boy."

Maisie thought for a bit longer then said,

"Mitchie's a girl, Miss Ellie. She just pretends she's a boy."

"Well! Now you have surprised me, Maisie. I never would have guessed it. She glanced towards the open back door, through which the sounds of Mitchie chopping wood came.

"How'd you work that one out? She had me completely fooled."

"It weren't hard to work out when she didn't have no clothes on, Miss Ellie."

Miss Ellie laughed. "You mean you were going to anyway, then found out?"

"Naaaaw! Miss Ellie, I made him.... her... wash. He wouldn't use the bathhouse so I said go in my room. I came in and saw her..." she grinned sideways.

Miss Ellie smiled and shook her head. "Well, you finally got what you wanted then." She'd have been very annoyed if it'd been one of her working girls who took up with another girl. That was as bad as falling in love with one of the customers, or getting religion – before you knew it they'd decide to quit whoring. Though she did know of some women that would carry on in this lucrative business and just amuse themselves on the side with a girl.

Just then Mitchie came back in with an armful of wood. She dropped it in the basket by the range, feeling Miss Ellie's eyes on her. She didn't know why she felt embarrassed, after all, this was a whorehouse. And this wasn't even like that, not whoring, Maisie was her girl. She squared her shoulders and looked back at Miss Ellie.

"Maisie tells me you're a girl," said Miss Ellie in a conversational tone.

Mitchie gulped and stared boggle-eyed at Maisie.

"What you go and tell her that for!?" she accused Maisie.

"I didn't see no harm in it, she got to know, you living here and all."

"No she don't! Ain't no business of anyone else!"

Mitchie was shocked at Maisie, betrayed already by her lover after only one day. She'd spent too much time being a boy to do anything like cry, but she stormed out, saying,

"I can't believe you done that!"

Maisie looked after her, astonished. She didn't think there was any harm in Miss Ellie knowing, why was Mitchie acting so crazy about it? Miss Ellie said,

"Stay here. I'll go talk to her." She was always having to settle some dispute or upset with her girls. She was quite good at it, which is why she ran a successful business. She found Mitchie by the pig-sty, still not crying, but hanging off the pig's fence with her head bent onto her hands. Miss Ellie came and stood by her, leaning against the fence. The pig came over and sniffed up at them, its mobile snout moving. Miss Ellie picked up the scratching stick and began to scrape the pig's back with it, just like any country girl. Mitchie straightened up and stood there, looking absolutely miserable.

"How long you been pretending to be a boy, Mitchie?" asked Miss Ellie.

"I guess around three years, Miss Ellie, ever since I run away from Mr Tranche back East. I didn't like him coming at me like he done, so I run away."

Miss Ellie nodded. Not an unusual tale, only the runaways more frequently ended up in brothels, or dead.

"You been working like that, with men, pretending you're a boy?" Mitchie nodded. Miss Ellie sighed and shook her head, "Mitchie, have you any idea what would happen to you if you ever got caught?

Mitchie nodded, "That's why no-one ever got to know, Maisie shouldn't 'a told you."

"No, Mitchie. That is why you got to stop doing it. I don't think you've got any idea what they'd do to you, out there with men who haven't seen a woman in months. There's no law would protect you."

She could tell from the look on Mitchie's face she didn't really know what she was talking about. "They'd rape you to death, Mitchie. That is not an easy way to die. It'd make what that Mr What's-his-name done to you seem like a picnic"

Mitchie glowered at her, still not wanting to believe her, but shaken anyway.

"I heard of it happening to some China-woman on the railways down in America. They tore her to pieces. You ain't seen that side o' men, Mitchie. You wouldn't be here if you had."

She could see she was getting through to Mitchie.

"Sweetie, Maisie done right to tell me. I'd have worked it out anyway. We all know Maisie likes girls better'n boys." She paused. "Stay here, Mitchie. You'll be safe here, you can help Maisie. God knows she needs it. If you shape up alright I'll pay you a proper wage."

The pig grunted, wanting her back scratched some more. Slowly Mitchie nodded. She didn't want to leave, she wanted to stay with Maisie.

"I ain't gonna do no whoring, though," she glared at Miss Ellie.

"No, Mitchie, I kind of figured that one out."

Mitchie lowered her hackles.

"I like working outdoors, Miss Ellie, but I'll help

Maisie too. I don't want to wear no dress though!" Miss Ellie considered this for a moment, then nodded agreement.

"Very well, but you watch yourself Mitchie." Mitchie nodded, knowing this already.

"And don't be fooling around with Maisie out in the open, you hear? Keep that inside her room. None of what we do goes out on the street, only inside, so none of them prying nosey parkers can complain."

Mitchie nodded again. Now her feeling of being betrayed by Maisie had gone. Suddenly Miss Ellie really was a princess to her, a queen. She might have fallen in love with her if she hadn't already been Maisie's girl. But from then on she saw Miss Ellie as her protector, a mother figure. She'd rescued Maisie and given her a proper home and now she'd rescued Mitchie. She'd have knelt and kissed her hand like someone from a story-book if she could have.

Miss Ellie gave one last scratch to the pig and beckoned Mitchie to follow her back to the house. When they got back to the kitchen

Mitchie noticed Maisie's face was kind of blotchy, like maybe she'd been crying. She stood there, awkward.

"Hey, I didn't mean to hurt your feelings none, Maisie." Maisie's mouth began to wobble.

"Miss Ellie says I got to stay and help you out some, so … I guess I'm staying." She wasn't sure how Maisie was taking it, but finally she smiled. They held hands a moment while the porridge glopped in the pot beside them on the range. Looking at them, Ellie was reminded of just how young they were. She knew Maisie was around 19, but Mitchie was surely younger. There wasn't a whore who hadn't thought herself in love at some time, Miss Ellie included. It always ended badly. She thought about McCabe. Maybe that never got completely burned out of you, no matter how sure you were it would never happen to you again.

Chapter 4

Eventually Miss Ellie did pass on to the other women that Mitchie was really a girl. They were a good bunch on the whole and she trusted them with something like this. They reacted with various kinds of amazement or amusement to this information. Somehow no-one ever got round to telling McCabe, who continued to think Mitchie was a boy, probably for the best.

Mitchie had actually received a very good training in cooking and housekeeping from Mr Tranche, so life improved for everyone when she started to help Maisie in the kitchen. It was good indoor work for winter.

The first falls of snow began to trickle down. The owner of the General stores did come and slaughter the pig, as Maisie'd predicted. They killed and bottled up most of the chickens too. When winter really got going there would be days on end when blizzards would be so bad no customers could make their way up to the house and everyone would sit round chatting, playing cards, painting toenails, sewing clothes and the like. Beryl would play classical music until the others told her to do something more cheerful. On busy nights, McCabe would get Mitchie to serve behind the bar. This was where they made their biggest profit; the women would entertain the customers and they would buy plenty of liquor. They would even sell meals to them if requested, now the cooking had improved enough not to put them off ever returning. Plenty of the men would even stay on after being with one of the women, drinking and playing cards. Dottie and Isabel would sometimes do a song and dance routine, with Beryl thumping out the tunes. Miss Ellie was doing her best to create a high-class place that offered a great night out for gentlemen, and they would flock in from far and wide for what was being offered, leaving poorer but happier.

Now that Mitchie had ambitions she had to think about learning a trade to keep her and

Maisie. She'd like to have been a carpenter, but knew she'd probably never get the chance to learn that, but she was learning fast here, so this would do.

Sometimes in the evenings, when she wasn't helping McCabe in the saloon, she'd lie beside Maisie, after they'd been making love, and talk about places she'd been and things she'd done in those three years as a boy. Whenever people talk like that it always makes drab and difficult experiences sound like great adventures, and Maisie never failed to be impressed. Mitchie's latent romantic streak began to take on a life of its own, and she'd talk about the future they were going to have together; what she would do for Maisie, in terms that were pure fantasy, but Maisie was delighted. She never thought her life would turn out so good after all the bad times.

When spring returned, the town returned to life. The sound of axes rang out in the forest around, and more new buildings were going up. There was talk of a new minister and his wife who came to the Presbyterians across the valley. Religion is always a popular form of entertainment in a culture devoid of theatres and concert halls, and of course is also open to women and children, as well as men, but its popularity did not seem to have any effect on business at Miss Ellie's establishment. The two of them - the church and the brothel – sat facing each other, across the small valley, each in its own way a focus for something in the new, struggling community, to lift hearts up out of the sweat and mud of mere existence to take a little pleasure and remember life was more than just toil.

Apparently the new Minister's wife believed greatly in doing good works and would go around helping anyone who was sick, and make collections of food for anyone who had fallen on really hard times. New people were moving in, there were some families now, people hoping to farm, not just mine, and other kinds of trades were setting up. Mitchie considered going to see if she could help out with some of the new building, she still had not forgotten her dream of becoming a carpenter, but there was plenty to do at Miss Ellie's. She was being paid wages now, and the free-and easy routine meant she and Maisie had plenty of time for each other.

Even though Miss Ellie had told them to confine their activities to the privacy of Maisie's bedroom, they could hardly resist kissing and holding hands when they were out back on the log smoking, or walking a little in the woods behind, but if anyone saw them, they thought Mitchie was a boy, so what did it matter?

They got a new pig in to fatten up for the next winter, and Mitchie built a bigger chicken coop, and got more hens in. Everyone could see Mitchie was really doing most of Maisie's work – Maisie was becoming more and more indolent- but as long as Mitchie was content with things, then it worked for everyone. There were some sour looks and mutterings from a couple of the women, if they saw the two girls acting too much like love-birds, but it was just in the normal ~~way~~ range of back-biting. The easy living and happiness was having an effect on Mitchie too. She began to fill out a little. She was now merely thin, not half-starved. Under the concealing men's clothes she developed a few curves and her face lost some of its angularity.

But then Maisie fell ill. She got a pain in her belly like cramps for her monthlies, but it wasn't that time. Then she was running a fever and threw up. They all thought it was a stomach cold, but the pain got worse. After a day it was clear there was more wrong than a normal stomach cold. Maisie was delirious and her belly seemed swollen well beyond its normal roundedness. She could not bear even a blanket over her, and screamed when Miss Ellie tried to feel her belly. Mitchie ran out to grab a passing child, gave him a penny and told him to go and get the doctor in. There *was* a doctor, of sorts, in the town – an old drunk – but he knew his stuff. It was raining heavily outside and everything had turned to mud. Mitchie sat by Maisie, bathing her face in cold water; the fever was burning her up and she was crying out in pain. It seemed to take an age and the doctor hadn't come. Finally, the bedraggled boy returned, but not with the doctor. He was off tending a mining accident and the boy couldn't find him. Instead, he brought in the Minister's wife, as she was known for tending the sick. By then, Mitchie was beside herself with fear. What was happening to Maisie? There was the Presbyterian woman in her black cloak, which she took off to reveal a stern-looking grey dress, buttoned up to the high collar – looking like everything Mitchie hated from her past. But she took one look at Maisie and rolled up her sleeves, ordered Mitchie to fetch some more water, and set to examining Maisie. Finally, someone who knew what they were doing! Mitchie ran off and re-filled the bowl of water. But before she got back in the lady had realized Maisie was dying of appendicitis. It had gone way beyond anything that anyone could do, even if they had caught it earlier, there was probably little chance Maisie could have survived the crude surgery that was all the doctor could have offered. He could set bones and deliver babies, but not much more. She saw the numb, disbelieving look on Mitchie's face as she explained this and thought *"That poor boy!"* She had expected, coming to such a den of iniquity as this, to find a debauched harlot, suffering some unnameable disease from her profession, realizing the terrible price she was paying for her life of sin and ready to repent on her deathbed, but instead, here were two young people, obviously servants of some kind, caught up in the same kind of tragedy as any ordinary folk. She wondered if they were brother and sister, in spite of the total lack of likeness to each other.

"My dear, my name is Sarah. I will sit with you. All we can do is give her laudanum and pray."

Miss Ellie came in and saw the situation, and bristled at the sight of this puritan woman, knowing her for her enemy. She listened to Sarah's prognosis and closed her eyes briefly and sighed.

"You gave her laudanum?" she asked Sarah,

who nodded, lips pursed at the sight of this woman with her hair all done up and her jewellery and scarlet dress and décolletage.

"There's no need for you to stay then, we can look after her."

Sarah was sitting on the only chair in the small room, and Mitchie was on the floor by Maisie's head, stroking her face and weeping. Sarah did not move and it was not possible for anyone to sit on the bed with Maisie - there was so little room and the slightest pressure was agony for her. The two women glared at each other and then Ellie turned and went to fetch another chair from the kitchen. There they sat, while the strains of music and drunken laughter and other noises filtered through from the saloon. Sarah began to read the Bible aloud, but Miss Ellie said,

"I'm grateful you have come here but I'll thank you to keep that cant out of here!"

They both looked at Mitchie, who could barely focus on anything. Sarah read silently after that. By morning Maisie was dead, and a numb, dazed Mitchie was taken off out of the way while Sarah and Miss Ellie washed Maisie and laid her out, as women have done since the dawn of time for the dead.

Mitchie sat, wrapped in a blanket, with Beryl by her side in the quiet saloon. Finally, when Maisie had been taken and Mitchie was absolutely beside herself, not knowing what to do with herself in her grief, Beryl took her up to her own room and dosed her up with some laudanum of her own, and Mitchie passed into a drugged sleep.

After they'd made all the arrangements for burying Maisie, Miss Ellie and Sarah stiffly bade each other farewell – their grudging acceptance of each other was still underscored with suspicion and judgement on both sides.

The funeral was held in the tiny graveyard next to the new chapel, that already had its share of graves, even so soon after it had been built. Even the most anti-religious person will want some sort of observance on the death of someone close, and all the women from the brothel attended. They clustered protectively around Mitchie. McCabe came late and stood at the rear. When Sarah saw Mitchie she came and took her hands, looking with concern at her white face and unfocussed, haunted eyes. Mitchie was grateful to her, and maybe she would have derived some comfort from it, but for one thing. When the Minister got up to start speaking she knew him. It was Mr Tranche. Sarah, that kind, good woman, was his wife.

Nearly four years had passed since Mitchie ran away from the Rev Mr Tranche. In that time she had grown taller, her shoulders were as broad as a boy's from the muscle she'd put on, her face was brown from all weather, and, above all, she was a boy to the public eye. Tranche did not give her a second glance.

How Mitchie managed to keep standing there at the graveside of all her hopes and dreams, with her worst nightmare standing only a few feet away, she wouldn't know. Beryl kept close by her side, her fingers wound into Mitchie's and holding her upper arm with her other hand. She felt Mitchie swaying, held her up while they filed outside, and helped her after. There was a surprisingly good turn-out, even though many of them had come just to gawk at the whores, rather than to give Maisie a send-off. Watching a whore get buried was good entertainment, almost as good as a hanging; seeing a bunch of women who still dressed shockingly, even in their funeral dresses, was a real treat and they didn't even have to pay for it.

They held a wake back in the saloon, but Mitchie stayed away. She went and sat out back with the pig for a couple of hours, scratching its back, then sitting down and leaning against the fence, just staring over the valley towards the church, whose little bell-tower she could just see through the roofs and trees of the small settlement. The pig lay down on its side of the fence, putting it back against hers, grunting contentedly, enjoying the company.

She wandered back in again when it began to get dark. A couple of the women were in the kitchen frying bacon and eggs. Miss Beryl came and pulled Mitchie in as she paused on the doorstep.

"I was worried about where you'd been. Come on now, sit here. Roxie, give her some food." They fussed her and made her eat. Miss Ellie came in from the saloon and crouched down in front to her to look in her face.

"I'll stay with her, Ellie. I got my monthly anyway, so I'd just as soon sit here," said Miss Beryl. Miss Ellie rubbed her face and nodded. She was exhausted too. There had been no break before the funeral, no reason to hold off, no relatives to wait for. She died in the night and was buried the next afternoon. The coffin-maker and gravedigger worked fast and Sarah Tranche made all the other arrangements.

"Miss Ellie!" Mitchie suddenly spoke, "I want to pay for Maisie's funeral. You ought not to go to the expense. I got some savings here. I should be the one to pay for it."

Miss Ellie shook her head.

"Sweetie, you don't have to do that. Maisie worked for us, we take care of that."

Mitchie looked stubborn.

"She was my girl. I was saving the money for her....." she tailed off, gulping back tears. "I was gonna get a ring."

The two women glanced at each other, but could think of nothing to say to that. Neither of them was going to say that Maisie was stupid to the point of not being quite right in the head, and she would have lived quite happily off Mitchie's devoted hard work for as long as she could. Mitchie was not in any state to hear that opinion. So Miss Ellie just said

"Mitchie, we all wanted to do the best we could for Maisie. You keep your money. It was the least we could do."

Mitchie continued to sit with Beryl on the battered two-seater, pulled up by the range. Beryl brought in a bottle of whiskey and they shared it. Mitchie was hoping for oblivion from the hooch, but it just made her feel more miserable. Without her knowing it, the wound of her mother's death had always lain there, unhealed, deep within. And now the death of her first love and the sudden reappearance of the man who she still believed had killed her mother, stirred an unbearable anguish in her. She never knew it was possible to feel so bad and yet still be alive. The pain was like an object inside her body, that couldn't be contained and no way of getting it out of her. Her mind prowled animal-like, seeking ease and finding none. So she drank. Beryl didn't try to stop her. She knew Mitchie would have to find a way to hang on and survive these next few months. Time heals, but that is no comfort until you've had the time. So Beryl just sat with Mitchie, holding her hand quietly.

Eventually Mitchie said,

"Miss Beryl, tomorrow I'm heading out of here. I gotta leave. I can't stay here."

"Sweetie, I know you feel that now, but you're in no fit state to go for a while. You stay here till you've had a chance to take in all in."

Mitchie stared at the floor.

"It ain't just Maisie, it's …." she tailed off. Suddenly it all just seemed too hard, her head couldn't hold all of this. She got up and went outside and threw up. Beryl followed and held her shoulders while she puked up everything, and stood there, leaning her arms against the wall. The last shudders of retching turned into sobs, and the tears finally began to flow. Beryl took her in, wiped her clean and wrapped her arms round her and rocked her till finally she'd got all the tears out – for the moment anyway.

Chapter 5

So, Mitchie stayed on. When she thought about going back to her old life, she realized she'd never be able to hack it. Having to act tough with other men while she was feeling the way she was, would be impossible. Here, the women all made a fuss of her, let her be if she felt bad and had to go off and cry a bit. They treated her like a kind of mascot. Prostitutes can be the most romantic women of all, even while reality is constantly grinding their noses in the prospects of ever finding a good man. At the back of even the most cynical mind there often gleams a little pink bubble of sentimentality. Mitchie's devoted grieving for someone the rest of them had regarded with tolerant amusement somehow touched them, even while they shook their heads and looked at each other in disbelief. McCabe still hadn't got that Mitchie was a girl, so he tried to give her some man-to-man advice. This did not go down well as man-talk consisted of telling her there were plenty more fish in the sea, and most of them weren't so fat and lazy. If Mitchie had any remaining thoughts of going back to live amongst men, that put an end to it.

Miss Ellie was only too pleased that Mitchie stayed. It was important to her business to keep her ladies happy. She'd worked in a few badly-run establishments, and knew the life from both sides. Having a reasonably good cook, who kept the place warm and clean and repaired was important. McCabe needed a hand around the place and they all needed a cook. Mitchie was perfect for both jobs, and her willingness and energy went down well too.

Sarah Tranche came over to visit Mitchie after the funeral. She felt great concern for this young man- a boy really – who was being exposed to such a life of sinful degradation. She had witnessed his grief at Maisie's death and felt it her duty to offer whatever consolation and help she could. She called round the back entrance, where she had come on her previous visit to Maisie's sickbed. Mitchie was sitting out back on the log, smoking. When she saw Sarah she flinched and didn't know where to look.

"Mitchie! How are you? Are you managing?"

"Yes, Miss Sarah, thank you."

"You know, we'd love to see you in chapel. You'd be most welcome."

Mitchie knew that tone – it was the same one they used when they talked about what a good man Rev Tranche was. She didn't say anything, just sat and looked down. There was an awkward silence, then,

"We all feel for you, dear Mitchie!" She really did sound kind. Mitchie nodded dumbly. Sarah came and perched beside Mitchie on the log.

"Erm... was Maisie your sister, Mitchie?"

"No, Miss Sarah, she was my girl."

"I see. Did you intend to marry her?"

"Yes'm ... only ...well …. " Mitchie hesitated for a long pause.

"You know Mitchie, it concerns me to see a young man like you in a place like this. It can come to no good. The Reverend Tranche and I could help you find work somewhere else. You could learn a trade, there are many opportunities for a keen young man like you." She waited, but could see she was not getting through to Mitchie.

"It's very kind of you, but I'm staying here. I got good work here and they treat me good."

There had been women, good women, like this around when Mitchie was a child. Determined to help, but utterly blind in their self-conviction to the dark evil that lay at the heart of their own church. Miss Ellie detested any religious people for the harm they could do her business, turning the heads of her ladies or mounting campaigns to have her closed down. But Mitchie's hatred was primitive, visceral, bone-deep, and even her awareness that Sarah was genuinely kind and meant her well, did not alter her instinctive reaction. She felt her jaw clamp shut. All those long years of not being allowed to speak out for fear of Mr Tranche, closed in on her. Fleetingly she wondered what had become of the picture of her mother she'd left under her pillow in the attic room when she ran away from him.

"Miss Sarah, I …. I'm grateful to you for all you done for Maisie, and seeing her buried decent and all, but you didn't ought to be coming out here. This ain't no place for you. You ain't really welcome. I'd thank you not to come again." She never knew where she found the strength to express even this modest rebuff, nor would Sarah Tranche know the courage it took to utter those words. But she saw something in Mitchie's face that told her she'd get nowhere, so she left.

Later, sitting at the dinner table with her husband, she talked of her day's work out in the community.

"What a shame! I'm sure that young Mitchie could really make something of himself. He seems such a nice boy.... something .." she searched for words, "...full of heart about him." Mr Tranche smiled indulgently at his wife for her sentimentality, while stuffing a forkful of liver and cabbage into his mouth. Sarah sighed, "But he would not speak to me. I fear he will waste his life far from the Lord. We must find ways to open the hearts of those people, but I declare I cannot think how.

Tranche grunted. "We must find ways to close the hearts of the townspeople against them, run them out of here!" He chewed noisily. Sarah pursed her lips. This was one habit she could never abide in him that he would eat in such a coarse way. "But we don't have enough influence here, yet. Too many of the miners prefer the house of iniquity to the house of the Lord. We would get nowhere if we spoke out against them."

One quiet day Mitchie was sitting in the saloon listening to Beryl play the piano.

"How'd you learn to play so pretty like that?" she asked. It was the Moonlight Sonata, and having had no experience of music apart from hymns, Mitchie thought it the most beautiful tune.

"My daddy taught me. He was a concert pianist."

Mitchie looked blank.

"He played the piano in concert halls and soirées for a living. We travelled all over, he was quite famous."

Mitchie blinked. "So how come you ended up here?"

"Oh, you know." Beryl shrugged, "my daddy drank too much. Things went bad. He died when I was twenty and ….well, this is how it turned out for me. It wasn't exactly the life I planned, but it's not a bad life. You get your freedom, more'n if you were married." she gave Mitchie a long look.

"You know, you're not bad-looking, Mitch, you'd do alright if you ever got a mind to try it."

Mitchie shook her head vehemently.

"No! No, I don't want to try it, Miss Beryl. I do alright the way I am."

Beryl nodded and smiled. "I guessed you'd say that." She turned back to the piano. "We like you being here, sweetie, you're helping keep this place running."

Mitchie glowed. No-one had ever said anything like that to her before.

Then Beryl started another tune, a burlesque one. Dottie and Isabel came in and started working on a new dance they were getting ready. They dragged Mitchie up and made her join in. Mitchie thought she'd never get something like that, but found she had a good sense of rhythm and managed at least not to step on anyone's feet. She was laughing by the time they finished. She went out back to get the food ready and realized, in spite of all she had believed, that life would go on, and maybe one day she'd feel good again. Beryl's eyes followed Mitchie as she left the saloon, noting the lightening of her manner, the softening of her face after the long shock of grieving.

"Not long now," she thought to herself. Her mouth quirked in the shadow of a smile. She went up to dress for the evening's work.

A couple of days later Mitchie was slinging a sack over her shoulder ready to go fetch some errands from the General Store. Beryl saw her and asked if she could see if they had any of the slim cigarillos she liked to smoke.

"Oh, and you'd better get me some tooth powder," she added, searching in her purse for some coins. She saw Mitchie get that momentarily glazed look that people get when they are memorizing something, and cocked her head.

"Mitchie, you could write a list you know. Did anyone ever teach you to read and write?"

"Yeah, I can do it some. My momma taught me afore she died, but I don't never need it. I can remember what I gotta get." She fished out her own tobacco and papers from her jacket. "You need a smoke to be going on with?"

Beryl took the tobacco and went and sat on the log, thinking, while she watched Mitchie stride off down the hill towards the town.

You could hear the clang and bustle of the place, the mooing of cattle being driven in, and a distant hoot of a steam engine from the mines. The church had been painted white now, its little bell-tower squatting on top of the square building, and the Minister's manse up above it almost as big as the church itself.

When Mitchie got back, Beryl found her and returned her baccy. She lit one of her own cigarillos and gave it to Mitchie for a puff. She took out a book. Mitchie knew she was a great reader and had a supply of books and she could read music too. Beryl said,

"Mitchie, you want to have a go at reading this? It's a good story, you'd like it."

Mitchie was startled.

"I can't do that, Miss Beryl. I don't read too good." She looked in alarm at the book.

"Give it a try. Here, I'll read out the beginning then you have a go after you've heard it."

She began to read. It was White Fang by Jack London. Mitchie shivered as Beryl read the opening description of a frozen, silent land and a string of sled dogs. Beryl stopped and took in Mitchie's rapt expression.

"You ever read a story book, Mitchie?"

"I ain't never read nothing but the Bible," she grimaced and looked down. "I 'member a story about a rabbit my momma used to get me to read."

Beryl smiled. "Yeah, I had that one too. Come on, try from here." She gave the book to Mitchie's reluctant hands and pointed a place for her to start. Stumbling, Mitchie worked out the words, one at a time.

"Down … the … frozen …" long pause, "waterway.. t-toiled... a. ..string... of..w-wolfish .. dogs." Once her mind had focussed itself she was amazed at how much she could remember. The Bible is full of long words and obscure phrases – so the simple immediacy of these words, describing things she knew and understood, caught her imagination. She looked up at Beryl with a bashful grin.

"Go on! You're doing fine, sweetie."

Mitchie continued on all the way down that paragraph, she even gained a little speed and fluency by the bottom of it, her grubby finger following the words written on the page. Beryl helped her with a few words, but she was surprised to see Mitchie really had a good grasp of it all.

"At front and rear, un.. unawed and in..in.. "

"Indomitable," supplied Beryl, "it means 'not beaten'." Mitchie nodded, "toiled the two men who were not yet dead." She understood that, and even though she didn't know the meaning of some of the words, she was thrilled by "Puny adventurers bent on colossal adventure, pitting themselves against the might of a world as remote and alien and pulseless as the abysses of space."

Beryl laughed gently at the look on Mitchie's face, "Keep it. I want to see you read it. It's a real boys' story, Mitchie, you'll enjoy it." She grinned.

"Thank you, Miss Beryl." Mitchie didn't know what to say. Just then McCabe called Mitchie to help him with the barrels and she ran off, leaving the book. Later she went to her room – Maisie's old room - and she found it placed on the wooden box of her bedside table, and on top of it, the story-book about the rabbit she remembered reading when she was little. She picked it up, sitting down on the bed, a huge lump came into her throat and her eyes filled, but she was touched deeply.

It was busy in the saloon early in the evening so Mitchie had to help McCabe. The ladies were all there, entertaining. It seemed like every time Mitchie looked up from her work, her eyes would meet Beryl's. Even when Beryl was taking a 'gentleman' upstairs her eyes kind of tracked across to Mitchie's.

It quietened down later and Mitchie went into her room. She took the rabbit book out and leafed through it, but the memories it aroused felt hard, so she put it away and took out White Fang. She read it for a couple of hours, finding it came easier and easier, gripped by the tale. Beryl had chosen well – it was a boy's story and she loved it.

When she turned in to sleep she had a vivid dream of being chased and lost, pursued by something terrifying but unable to escape because she had left something precious back somewhere and had to go back for it. There was a terrible smell in the dream that filled her senses. Suddenly the sound of the door opening penetrated the dream and she surfaced. Someone was coming into her room, carrying a candle. Still half in the dream, she flung herself into the corner of her bed by the wall, whimpering "No! No!"

The shape came and put the candle on the box and turned to her, and there was Beryl, sitting on the bed and saying,

"It's only me, Mitchie. Hey, I'm sorry, I didn't mean to scare you."

Mitchie focussed and surfaced completely from the dream.

"It's alright Miss Beryl. I was just having a bad dream." She relaxed.

Beryl reached out to her and Mitchie just fell into her arms. As their lips met and Beryl's light perfume filled Mitchie's senses she had a flash of the terrible smell in her dream. She realized what it was, the smell and taste of Mr Tranche's foul breath combined with the sickly pomade he used on his hair. But now, Beryl's mouth tasted sweet, of makeup and perfume and just the taste of her. Mitchie's arms were round Beryl's neck, holding on to her tight. Beryl's hands pulled up the men's undershirt Mitchie wore in bed, found her breasts, and squeezed her nipples as she kissed Mitchie. Mitchie's whole body thrilled. Beryl was pulling the undershirt up, trying to get it off Mitchie. Their mouths came apart long enough for Mitchie to rip it off herself, then she flung herself back at Beryl. Beryl pushed her down on her back and pulled at her long men's underpants.

"Take these off!" she whispered into Mitchie's mouth, then she sat up and unwrapped her housecoat from herself. Mitchie wriggled the long pants off herself, her eyes on Beryl. She must have been all of thirty, maybe even as old as forty, Mitchie couldn't tell, but her body was tight and lithe. Mitchie remembered something in the Bible about breasts like pomegranates- she didn't know what a pomegranate looked like, but she thought it a lovely word for Beryl's breasts. She reached out. Beryl took her hands and pushed them up above Mitchie's head, against the bed-head, and lay on top of her, her lips meeting Mitchie's again. Her skin was like satin and slid over Mitchie. She continued to hold Mitchie's wrists with one hand while the other glided over Mitchie, touching her breast, squeezing it, her lips came down to suck on that little apple while her hands continued down to Mitchie's ass. She cupped one cheek, her fingers slipping into the crevice between them, and squeezed hard, biting gently on Mitchie's nipple. Mitchie breathed a groan and tried to move her hands to take and stroke Beryl, but Beryl stiffened her hold on her wrists, held them there.

She kissed Mitchie again, her lips hot from her breast, and said,

"You just lay there, honey, let me do it all."

Her hand went down to Mitchie's cleft, parted her and skilfully found her way in. Her fingers glided in the warm wetness, exploring, testing. Her hair brushed Mitchie's face and chest, enveloping her, her lips hovering in Mitchie's breath as her hand did its work. The tip of one finger found its way right into Mitchie, pushed deeper, pulled out and thrust again. A few more thrusts and Mitchie was pushing herself at Beryl's hand, ready for her to start using her mouth down there, like her and Maisie always used to do. But Beryl took her hand away and sat up. She took something from the pocket of her robe and opened it, a small bottle of fine oil. She poured some on her hands, smoothed it over and added more to her fingers. She looked over and smiled at Mitchie, who lay with her hands still holding the end of the bed, watching, her breath shallow and fast. Beryl turned back to Mitchie's pussy and slid three of her fingers right in - they went in easily, oiled and scented. Mitchie gasped a little and opened her legs. Beryl was still sitting, half leaning over Mitchie, her eyes on Mitchie's face, her tongue caressing her own lip as she smiled and thrust in further. She could see the surprise on Mitchie's face.

"Am I hurting you?"

Mitchie panted and shook her head.

"No.. just .. Maisie never done that."

"Well, this is how I like it." Beryl thrust in and out of the hot cavern of Mitchie's widening pussy. Her breath was coming ragged too now, like Mitchie's and a sheen of perspiration slicked her skin. Further in, picking up the moisture from inside and sliding it out and across Mitchie's sweet spot and back in again. More fingers, squeezing in, stretching Mitchie, a sweet, swift-passing pain. Mitchie's mind flitted to a memory of seeing Beryl cutting her nails earlier that day. She'd thought she kept them short to play the piano!

She was pushing herself onto Beryl's hand, her ass clenching and lifting from the bed. The sensation was intense, she was utterly open to this beautiful woman, utterly filled by her. The feeling grew and rose up in her, so big she could hardly contain it, could hardly get enough of it. Beryl's elbow and shoulder were moving in rhythm with each thrust, she had closed her eyes, sensitive to every movement and response of Mitchie's body, playing her like an artist. Now! The moment she'd waited for! She was sure she was ready. Mitchie was almost sobbing her passion, giving herself utterly to Beryl. She straightened her fingers and brought them all together and carefully, firmly thrust right in, all of her fingers delving in, up to the knuckles, deeper now, the knuckles hesitating on that narrow place, feeling it widen, open, and yes! She was in! Her whole hand slid in and was completely inside Mitchie, buried so far Mitchie could feel it in her ass. She cried out, disbelieving and looked down at Beryl's wrist enveloped in the folds of her pussy. She looked at Beryl with wide, scared eyes. Beryl gasped "Oh you sweet thing!" and thrust in again. She noticed Mitchie's look and whispered, "Sh-sh-sh! It's all right, I won't hurt you, you can take it."

They breathed and sobbed and gasped

together, building and building, Mitchie thought she would swell and burst with the pleasure of it. She bit her forearm to stifle the shout of ecstasy. She was like a strung bow, only her feet and upper back lay on the bed as she lifted herself up towards – around - Beryl's pumping hand. She writhed and groaned, fists clenched around the iron bars of the bed-head. She came in such a sharp spasm a rush of fluid poured from her. She came on and on, clenching and loosening around Beryl's hand, her moans and muffled cries keeping time with what Beryl was feeling through her hand. Beryl was moaning too, the reverberations of Mitchie's abandoned response transmitted to her own pussy. What a little peach of a girl!

Finally she felt the pulse slow and still. Carefully, she extracted her hand, and lay herself back along the length of Mitchie, pressing herself into her mound, allowing herself a final thrust and inner quiver, before she too quietened.

Propping herself on her elbow, she pushed her hair from her face to look at Mitchie. Now she allowed Mitchie to put her arms around her. Mitchie hugged her and whispered,

"I love you so much! I feel bad saying that, coz of Maisie, but I do, I love you!"

Beryl kissed her softly.

"You give your heart so easily!" her eyes were soft and concerned.

"Am I bad to?" asked Mitchie.

"Oh, no, Mitchie! You are sweet and loving." She leant her forehead against Mitchie's, her hair tumbling down like a tent around them. "There's nothing bad about it."

They lay like that, quiet, still, lips just touching, breathing into each other, for a long exquisite moment until finally Beryl slid off Mitchie and held her, pulling the blanket up over them both. Beryl just lay there, smiling at Mitchie. Mitchie didn't think she'd ever seen anyone so beautiful. Eventually she said

"I ain't never done it like that. Maisie just used to ..." she tailed off.

"Yum-yum" Beryl finished her sentence,

nodding.

"You knew that? Did you ever go with Maisie?"

Beryl laughed and shook her head, "No, Mitchie, I did not ever go with Maisie." She propped her head on her hand, pushing her hair back with the other hand. "But Maisie did ask most of us. We all knew what she liked."

Mitchie grimaced. "I guess no-one liked her the way I did."

Beryl didn't want to hurt Mitchie's feelings, so she said, "Well I am the only one of us who likes girls too, and … well …. Maisie was a little too much woman for me." She smiled at Mitchie. "I like a boy-girl like you."

Mitchie smiled shyly back.

"Yeah, I guess she was quite a lot of woman, weren't she?"

"She was indeed."

Mitchie suddenly realized what she'd been saying.

"Oh! I'm sorry, you don't want to hear me talk about her!"

"It's alright. You don't have to say sorry."

They wrapped themselves around each other and lay quiet again. Beryl was thinking.

"Mitchie, have you ever been with a man? Did you go with any of the men out there working with them?"

Mitchie was startled by the question.

"No, they never knew I was a girl," she hesitated. "It was before … that's why I ran away. " She stopped.

"Tell me."

Slowly, with the help of Beryl's questioning, Mitchie told it all.

"Mr Tranche?!" Beryl exclaimed.

"Yeah."

"When did you first realize he'd come here?"

"At the funeral. He weren't married back then. I never saw that Sarah before."

"Oh my dear! So you had that to deal with on top of Maisie's dying!"

Mitchie nodded. Beryl puffed out a long breath.

"No wonder you wanted to get away!"

"Yeah", Mitchie whispered, suddenly overwhelmed by this thing that she had been pushing out of her mind in the months since Maisie died.

"Do you think he recognized you?"

Mitchie shook her head.

"I watched him when we was at the grave," she paused and swallowed, "he never even looked at me. I kept my head down so's he wouldn't notice me."

She shivered, suddenly covered in goose bumps. Beryl noticed immediately.

"Oh Sweetie! I'm sorry. I never meant to stir you up asking you this!" She pulled the blanket tightly around Mitchie and held her. Mitchie cuddled into her.

"But I'm glad you told me. You shouldn't have to bear that alone."

For Mitchie, after a lifetime of indifference from others for her suffering, Beryl's attention was like rain in a desert. After all, she'd even mentioned this to Miss Ellie, and she'd brushed it aside, and had forgotten Tranche's name, seeing it as yet another everyday tale of many girls of Mitchie's class.

But Beryl, while aware there was nothing unique about Mitchie's tale – especially in women of her profession – was coldly enraged by the story. She stored away the information, but knew there was nothing to be done about it. She sighed. She wanted to hold onto Mitchie, shelter her, but she needed to get back to her own bed.

"Baby, I got to go now, gotta get some beauty sleep." she cupped Mitchie's face with her hand. "You be ok now? On your own?"

Mitchie nodded. Beryl kissed her softly.

"We got to keep this to ourselves, you hear? Ellie wouldn't be happy if she knew I was seeing you," she grinned. Mitchie nodded.

"I won't say nothing."

Beryl slipped out of the rough little bed and pulled on her robe. She gave Mitchie one last kiss and, taking her candle, left quietly and made her way back up to her own room.

Mitchie lay for a long time awake, filled with mixed feelings, most of them delightful.

She looked back at what she'd been like when she first arrived at Miss Ellie's, was it eighteen months ago? Longer? And everything she'd been through since, and she saw how changed she was. Before, she'd been almost feral, guarded, detached, even though she could put on the charm when she needed to. Now, things had opened up in her. Being in love with Maisie had opened a window inside, and now this beautiful, mature, cultured woman taking an interest in her was overwhelming. Beryl could have asked her to jump through fire and she'd have done it.

Chapter 6

Mitchie did manage to keep everything under wraps this time – not like when she was with Maisie. She didn't want to let Beryl down or upset anything in the running of this place that was her whole security. She took her lead from Beryl. If she came over to sit with her, to see how her reading was progressing or whatever, Mitchie went with that and pretended everything was just as normal. So no-one saw anything out of the ordinary in the way the two of them behaved.

But Mitchie got an insight into why Beryl was so careful of Miss Ellie, one day when she had been laughing and joking with Dottie and Isabel while they gave her another dancing lesson. She liked them and enjoyed the teasing they gave her over her attempts to learn their routines. She was dancing with her hands on Dottie's hips and trying to wiggle her own ass too and gave Isabel a cheeky grin and waggled her eyebrows suggestively while she pretended to put her hands right on Dottie's ass- as she had seen the men do. Ellie saw this and frowned. Later she took Mitchie aside and told her in no uncertain terms not to try anything with any of the women.

"It was alright with Maisie, but you try and turn any of my ladies and you'll be out of here, you hear?"

Mitchie nodded, genuinely surprised.

"I weren't doing nothing, Miss Ellie, we was just fooling. I wouldn't … " She stopped. She was so glad Beryl was nowhere in sight, her eyes would surely have gone to her, betrayed her. "I wouldn't do nothing like that," she finished.

Miss Ellie's voice softened. "You're a good worker, Mitchie, and I'm glad of your help round here, but things have a way of happening. Just watch yourself. You turn any of them and they decide they want to leave the business, you could ruin everything just as it's going good."

This was a heavy load of responsibility to put on Mitchie, and Beryl was indignant when she told her.

"She should know better'n that, she's been around in this business as long as I have," she said.

"What did she mean 'turn'? Like, to turn from liking men to liking girls?"

"Uh-huh." Beryl nodded, smiling at Mitchie. Mitchie grinned back.

"Did I turn you?"

Beryl had a way of laughing in her throat without really opening her mouth that Mitchie loved. She kissed Mitchie and said

"Turned my head, maybe. The rest of me was already well and truly turned."

Mitchie couldn't kiss her back properly for smiling.

Beryl couldn't come down to Mitchie every night. Sometimes she'd just had too many gentlemen to see, and she would need to be alone. The men were alright, she didn't dislike sex with them, but too many of them left her feeling like she had sand under her skin, like a cat with its fur rubbed the wrong way. So she'd stay in her own bed. It was quite a claustrophobic life in many ways, little privacy inside the house and hard to just walk around outside in the settlement without attracting the wrong kind of attention. The only right kind being the kind that paid.

One night when it had been busy, Mitchie lay in her bed, waiting for Beryl but not really expecting her. Everything was quiet in the house, outside the moon was full. Roxie always said that made everyone crazy and horny. She believed everything like that, told their fortunes with cards, looked at tea-leaves, and that kind of thing. Mitchie didn't know about any of that but she sure was horny. She reached over to the small bottle of oil that Beryl kept in her room and opened it. She sniffed it. The scent reminded her of Beryl, of all they did together, Beryl's slender, strong hands on her, in her, knowing exactly where to touch and slide and thrust, prolonging it, hastening it, sometimes hurting but always driving Mitchie, pushing her to heights of sensation, each time it felt new even as her hands found familiar pathways. Mitchie was eager, like putty in her hands, Beryl would play her, delighting in her responsiveness. Mitchie tipped the bottle and let some of the oil onto her fingers, then put the bottle back and lay down. She spread her legs and slid her oiled fingers into herself. She knew what she was doing this time. She circled round her sweet spot, building the feeling, dreaming of fingers and tongue on her. She dipped down into the depth below then out and up to that place. She began to work herself hard now, splayed herself out, blanket thrown off so she could look at herself. She pinched her nipple and pulled on it, that small pain adding to the build and spread of delicious pulsing sensation.

The door of her room opened and Beryl came in, her candle fluttering in the movement of air. Her eyes lit on Mitchie in full flow with herself and she grinned.

"Couldn't wait for me?" she chuckled, placing the candle near the glowing lamp. Mitchie stilled her fingers.

"Thought you wouldn't come tonight." She didn't know whether to be embarrassed. Maybe it was disloyal of her to do this, like being unfaithful or something. Beryl sat on the edge of the bed.

"Go on," she said, "keep going." Her tongue flicked along her lower lip, "Let me watch."

Mitchie felt shy all of a sudden. Beryl laid her own hand on Mitchie's in its nest of flesh. Mitchie started moving her fingers again. She almost had to go back to the beginning with herself, but there it was!

Beryl's eyes travelled along Mitchie's body, flicked up to her face, a little smile on parted lips, then returned to the working hand, brown against the white of Mitchie's thighs and belly.

"Harder now! Come on, do it for me!" breathed Beryl.

Mitchie was longing for Beryl to touch her, take her but she didn't put a finger on her, had not even unwrapped the body Mitchie adored from her robe. But the look on Beryl's face spurred Mitchie on, spurts of pleasure began to shoot and spread from her groin, to build and fall and rise again. She could see Beryl's breathing change, her face rapt, urging Mitchie on, and her own breath caught, held and released. She arched a little, her head falling back, eyes closing. There! Again! Oh yes! It's coming! She looked again at Beryl, bent now over Mitchie's pulsing centre, almost as if she was smelling the hot scent rising from it, urging Mitchie on. She closed her eyes and rode the wave of it all the way up, longing in the last breaking of it for Beryl to be in her, gasping as she climaxed, a little more! Yes! A small groan and more! Her ass tensed and she pushed up from the bed, and there! All of it now!

She subsided, laying there, panting a little and watching Beryl through half-closed eyes. She breathed deeply and grinned sideways at Mitchie. She leant over her, opening her robe as last,

"Mmm! You come so beautifully!" She slid herself out of her robe and took Mitchie's hand from her crotch, licked the fingers, sucked them, a wicked glint in her eyes. She made her mind up.

"Turn over." Unsure, but willing, Mitchie began to turn.

"Right over, on your belly, there now, yes." Her hands pushed Mitchie into position. She ran her fingers along the crack of Mitchie's ass, let them linger over the centre place. Mitchie was surprised to feel a pleasant flutter of response. Beryl hovered and stroked in that place, playing gently with Mitchie, watching her response, seeing Mitchie's inward gaze on the side of her face she had turned towards her on the pillow, assessing this new experience.

"Play with yourself again," she commanded. Surprised, Mitchie put her hand down into the swollen dampness. She watched, face side on in the pillow, as Beryl oiled her hand carefully, then leant over, parted her ass-cheeks and tipped a little extra oil right into the crack. What was she going to do? Mitchie felt the oil pool and trickle and a ripple passed through her groin and belly. Then Beryl began to rub her fingers around the entrance of her ass-hole.

Carefully she slid one finger in and out of the tight opening. Mitchie felt strangely vulnerable, her finger unmoving on her clit, she took in this new sensation.

Beryl continued. Two fingers, dipping in and out, waiting, sensing Mitchie's response, massaging around the entrance, the oil she had applied combining with the juices that had run down from Mitchie's own earlier pleasuring of herself. This was so new, but it felt like it did round the front. Mitchie's initial uncertainty evaporated. Beryl was showing her a new secret of her body. Trustingly, she followed wherever Beryl was taking her.

Deeper now, the fingers delved and probed, sensing, holding back, coming in again, and now! Yes! In a rush of sensation, Mitchie felt herself open further. Suddenly her whole body cried out to be entered, penetrated, she gasped and Beryl's fingers slid right into her.

"Mmhh! Good girl!" whispered Beryl and began to push hard into Mitchie. She added the rest of her fingers. It hurt a little but Mitchie didn't care – this was bliss, let Beryl fuck her blind, let her hurt her, let her do anything as long as she didn't stop!

Beryl's expression was intent, almost hard as she abandoned herself to her pleasure. Mitchie was her toy, her slave in this moment. She wanted to possess her utterly, and she did. Oh how Mitchie was responding! Now her hand underneath her was working furiously on herself.

"Yes! Go!" panted Beryl, pushing harder and faster into Mitchie. She groaned, Mitchie groaned too, panting, biting her lip to hold in a cry, "More! I want more!" she spread her legs and arched her back, Beryl was stretching her hard now, every part of her – inside and out – pulsed with waves of sensation. Deep inside, her vagina rang out like a deep bell in unison with the waves of climax from her ass. She came so hard she pissed herself a little. Beryl, too, kneeling over Mitchie, felt her own inner thighs wet as Mitchie came and came again under her. For a long, long moment both of them flew together through eternity, until the tide receded, and they were back in time, and now it was dying embers of a hearth fire, a leaf floating gently down in the warm air, a descent into quietness and completion. Mitchie felt the fall of Beryl's hair on her sweating back, a brief touch of lips, then Beryl gently pulled her fingers out of her. She rose and went to the washstand. Mitchie lay, a pooled liquid on the bed, unmoving, listening to the sounds of Beryl washing. Then she turned and opened her arms to Beryl when she softly returned to the bed. They lay together, too close for words. They drowsed. Beryl did not want to leave, but finally she pulled herself awake and softly crept from the room while Mitchie slept.

Dawn light was glimmering as Beryl quietly climbed the stairs to her own room. She still glowed inside from the pleasure she'd had with Mitchie. Adroitly, she picked her way avoiding the creaking boards, but just as she opened her door, Ellie's bedroom door opened and the two women halted, both surprised. Ellie's eyes narrowed, but Beryl just nodded briefly and continued into her room. There was a pause, then Ellie pushed into Beryl's room. Her instincts were aroused. There is an entirely different look on the face of someone who has been sitting in a cold kitchen suffering from insomnia to that on the face of one who has just risen from her lover's bed. Ellie had known Beryl off and on for many years, but found her aloof as a cat, always poised. She looked up at Ellie now from her place sitting on her bed, holding a cigarillo ready to light. Intuitively Ellie got it, she nodded,

"You been with Mitchie, haven't you? Is that where you been?"

Beryl lit her cigarillo and swung her feet up onto the bed.

"What difference does it make if I have?"

"You know I don't like my ladies doing with each other, not unless it's for show."

Beryl drew on her smoke and looked at Ellie, considering her reply.

"Ellie, I've always had a girl on the side, if I could. Didn't you know I used to go with that little Valentina when we were back in Quebec City?" She shrugged. "It doesn't stop me working. Men are business, girls are pleasure, what's the problem?

Ellie was surprised. "I didn't know that. I didn't know you were that way inclined."

"Well, don't you worry about me, Ellie, I don't create waves. You're a good business woman and I'm a good whore," she smiled. "Besides, you're a fine one to talk. Look at you with McCabe. You're really playing with fire there."

Ellie's face changed. She sighed and nodded.

"I guess. I trust you to keep things discrete, Beryl. You know the score as well as I do." Beryl inclined her head, graciously.

"You too, dear."

Ellie nodded and left. Beryl finished her smoke and lay down to catch some sleep.

Ellie went down to the kitchen. She looked at Mitchie's door, with its cut-out moon shape. Who expected that room to get so much action when they built it for Maisie?

She sat on the old two-seater by the range, restless. Beryl was right. Getting involved with McCabe had not been part of her plan, definitely not! But even when her head was telling her this was such a bad idea, her hormones had taken over and pushed all that aside. Of course, he'd expected that as part of the deal ever since they set up their business, but she'd kept him off. How long? It must be over three years since they built the house and started the business. She'd only approached him to work with her in the first place because he was running that apology for a brothel, with the three girls in tents, when she arrived in the settlement. She could see the potential for a well-run business as soon as she'd got there and had talked McCabe into giving up what he already had, to go into creating a real classy place with her.

And now, after all that time, she'd had one moment of weakness, of needing someone to be there, and she forgot all her common sense.

Now she knew she'd somehow lost the upper hand. Men were always like that. She hardly ever had sex with any of the gentlemen herself, her job was to run the place, not be part of the merchandise, but occasionally the need might arise, and she knew McCabe would make trouble about that. And he would now think all the money they made was theirs together, which meant, his, and that could only lead to problems in the future. You just couldn't mix business with pleasure, Beryl certainly had that right, and emotional connections of any kind just entangled you in crazy webs of need and expectation. She sighed. Dammit! Why did she have to like him so much? She couldn't plan her way forward on this one – she just had to take it as it came.

They had a good thing going here, money was rolling in. Men came from far and wide, attracted to the honey-pot she offered. It was a man's world out here and she catered to it.

She sighed. Maybe it made no difference if she slept with McCabe anyway. Most of the customers assumed she and McCabe were together, they wouldn't expect anything else of a man and a woman running a business together. Ellie just hated the thought of being perceived as belonging to any man, of losing her autonomy.

She got up and put more wood in the stove, filled the black kettle and put it on to boil. She opened the back door and looked out, smelled the air. Getting cold! Fall was here. It'd soon be time to kill the hog again. She went to look for eggs in the chicken coop.

Beryl told Mitchie that Ellie knew about them now. Mitchie was worried.

"She told me she'd throw me out if I went with any of you ladies."

"No, I put her right on that. I thought she knew I had a girl back in Quebec City. Turns out she never realised."

Mitchie took in this new information.

"How come you left her?" she asked.

Beryl looked sad a moment, then grimaced.

"She was a little too fond of opium. A lot of them do it in this business, sometimes you just want to block it all out. But she, well, she just went too far. Got so she wasn't interested in anything else really, not even me." she pursed her lips then looked sideways at Mitchie. "So, we've both had our hearts broken before, hmm?"

Mitchie nodded, eyes soft on her lover's face. "We got each other now."

"Yes", and Beryl leant over to kiss her.

Chapter 7

Winter came and blizzards kept people in their homes. Some of the women went back East before all the trails closed down. The winters here could drive you crazy. Cities never had quiet times, they were always open for business. But Beryl didn't go, even though she chafed at the confined life they led here. She didn't want the temptations life in the city would offer, expensive temptations. She hoarded her money, saving it for a future that did not involve whoring. With fewer women, there was more money to be made when the clients could get through.

On fine days, when the snow lay deep, she'd go out with Mitchie. They'd walk and talk. Sometimes all of them would go out and throw snowballs and laugh and scream, their cheeks red and noses running in the frozen air. Beryl gave Mitchie an old quilt of hers to keep warm at night, and persuaded her to use sheets on the bed too, something she'd never had in her life.

The others were aware she'd taken Mitchie under her wing a bit, but they all made something of a pet of her. The fact that she still looked like a boy and was so young, endeared her to them, made them all a little protective.

Mitchie basked in it. She read everything she could get from Beryl, though she gave up quickly on the poetry, and the obscure wordiness of Shakespeare baffled her.

Sarah Tranche had never returned to the brothel to see Mitchie, but she did see her around the township, running errands, and would greet her, asking how she was whenever she could. She always got the same answer,

"I'm doing fine, Miss Sarah, thank you for asking."

Only once did this happen when Sarah was accompanied by Rev Tranche, and then Mitchie just ducked away, clearly unwilling to meet them. Sarah turned to her husband,

"There goes that boy, Mitchie. Do you remember him from Maisie's funeral?"

Tranche looked after Mitchie and shook his head. "I did not see him on that day, only that nest of vipers that accompanied him. And McCabe. How a man can allow himself such iniquity! Some will stop at nothing to make a dollar, delving into the depths of depravity as deeply as these honest working men delve into the bowels of the earth for the precious gifts left there by our Creator!"

These words made a favourable impression on those who stood around, listening. The settlement was becoming a regular town year by year, with more women and children appearing. And they were not comfortable to be cheek-by-jowl with an infamous house.

A Cree band moved near the settlement. The winter was harsh and they were starving. The Tranches made much of their Christian charity, providing food and blankets for them. But they demanded a price by making them come and listen to Tranche preach – not in the chapel, which was for white folks – but in a tent put up for the purpose.

When a couple of the Cree appeared at the back door of Miss Ellie's, they gave too, but did not feel the need to blow a trumpet about it. But then McCabe set up a deal with some of the Cree men to trade furs for booze. No-one at the time understood the native inability to metabolize alcohol in the way Europeans could, but they knew enough about 'drunken Indians' to know McCabe was making trouble by his actions. Ellie quarrelled bitterly with him about this, but he insisted he knew what he was doing, was cocky in his self-belief. Ellie fumed, sensing trouble, frustrated at being tied to McCabe, even while she still took him to her bed.

The thaw came and the year moved into summer. Some of the women returned from the City, a couple didn't but a couple of new ones came in. More settlers came in, still mainly men, looking to make money mining, but also some regular families. It was easier now to get timber to build a house from the sawmill, if you had the money to pay for it. The covered wagons and the tents of the newly arrived were quickly transformed into small wooden shacks and cabins. Rough men still made up the bulk of the population, but the balance was shifting.

The Cree band had moved off when the thaw came, but some lingered in the area. They continued to trade in furs and skins for booze, and their crazy drunkenness added to the sense of disorder. A couple of their women were hanging around the miners' shacks, selling themselves. Miss Ellie was not pleased – the miners may have been coarse, but they had money, they were the backbone of her trade, and she didn't want competition. But there was no way she'd bring those women into the house to work for her – she didn't mind helping them out with food in the winter, but she had standards. Flossie was rumoured to be mulatto, that was exotic enough and did attract some custom, but she drew the line at

Indians.

McCabe had always had a good working relationship with Art Skinner and his brother Joe, the owners of the General Store in the settlement. But now he quarrelled with them over selling booze to the Cree. Ellie too wanted him to stop stirring up trouble by doing this. He agreed, but his quarrel with Skinner had riled him up and he began to import his own liquor, by-passing Skinner and even setting up a still back in the woods.

Time passed.

One day, in the height of summer, Mitchie was making her way along by the river to the store. The heat shimmered and flies buzzed. A bald eagle took off from the dead top of a pine and rose up on the warm currents to hover in the blue sky, making its small mewling call. It was the kind of day that made you feel glad to be alive. Some boys were down in the river swimming. There was a good deep bit there, not too swift and they were plunging in from a rock that jutted over the pool. Some of these boys were new in, but Mitchie recognized a couple of miner's sons. She couldn't help slowing a little, to watch them, envious of their freedom to swim like that, stark naked in the cold water.

One of them saw her and raised his arm from the water.

"Hey, why'n't you come on in?" he called.

The others turned to look. Mitchie grinned and shook her head in negation.

"Naah! I got chores to do," she waved and backed off. She heard one of them say, "That's the boy lives in the …." the last word was whispered. The boys laughed. Then she heard footsteps running behind her and turned. The biggest boy, maybe fifteen, already strong and muscular, came up, dripping river water, his cock shrivelled from the cold mountain water.

"Hey!" he called out, "What's the matter with

you? How come you never play with us?"

Mitchie backed off. "I .. I gotta go do chores and stuff."

"So? I got chores too." he laughed. The other boys came up.

"Come on! You got time for a swim, it's good in there." The other boys grinned, their eyes curious.

Mitchie was embarrassed by the sight of these naked boys. She didn't want to look at all those cocks, no matter they were all pretty inoffensive. The boy saw her embarrassment and his eyes narrowed.

"Hey, you scared to get undressed out here? You ain't a Jew boy, are you? Is that what it is, eh? You been cut? You scared we'll see?"

"I ain't a Jew boy, I just don't wanna..." Mitchie turned and ran. That was a signal for the big boy to scream "Get 'im!" and they all gave chase. Mitchie could run fast but she was a little out of practice after the easy life at Miss Ellie's and the boys were strong and agile.

They jumped on her and pulled her down.

"Jew boy! Let's see the Jew boy pisser!" shouted out the older boy. The other boys had no idea really what they were meant to be looking at, but they joined in.

"Jew boy! Jew boy!" they cried, and while Mitchie fought and struggled, their hands pulled at her pants, dragging them down and her underpants too. They were crowded in so close, pushing each other and hanging on to her arms and legs, at first none of them could see past each other. But the oldest boy pulled her shirt flap aside, tearing it and then stopped. One of the boys said in a high frightened voice,

"They cut it right off? I didn't know they cut it right off like that!"

"Lemme see! Lemme see! What is it?"

The oldest boy said, "It ain't cut. That's a pussy, that is. He ain't a boy. He got a pussy. That's a girl!"

They were so astonished Mitchie managed to get herself free. She kicked the big boy hard in his crotch, and ran like a hare, holding her pants up. She ran into the forest, leaping on the large, moss-covered boulders and fallen trees. Fear gave her feet wings and somehow she never lost her footing. The boys began to give chase, but the boy she'd kicked called them back.

"Leave 'im .. her ..We know where 'e lives. I'm gonna tell my Dad 'bout this." He glared after Mitchie, hatred in his eyes, then turned and ran for his clothes.

Mitchie burst into the back door of Miss Ellie's, panting, sweat-soaked and dishevelled. Most of the women were in the kitchen, chatting, eating, smoking, the usual afternoon lull. Mitchie staggered to her knees and knelt there panting. Beryl ran over to her and the others crowded behind.

"Mitchie! What is it?"

"I gotta get out of here! I gotta go quick!" She began to get up, "They found out about me. I gotta go." She tried to push towards her room door, but Beryl grabbed her,

"What do you mean? Tell me!"

"They know I'm a girl! They gonna kill me!"

Beryl shook her. "What happened? Tell us, Mitchie, come on, calm down!"

Mitchie wiped her face and fought back tears. She had already reverted to the half feral child she'd been when she arrived over two years before, but being a girl for that time, meant she had re-learnt how to cry.

"Did some of the men get at you?"

"No, it was kids, them boys. They thought I was a Jew boy coz I didn't wanna swim with them. They wanted to see if my pecker was cut."

Mitchie was pushing past Beryl, still saying "I gotta get outta here. They was running to tell. That McKinnon boy, his pa's foreman down there."

The women were all talking at once, shouting over each other. Beryl still had hold of Mitchie. She shouted out, "Quiet! All of you!"

They all stopped and looked. In the sudden silence McCabe's voice came out loud,

"Mitchie's a girl?! How come no-one told me?" He pushed his hat back on his head and scratched, glaring at Ellie. She sighed, exasperated and said

"We'll talk later."

Beryl looked into Mitchie's face, made her focus on her and said,

"Mitch, it's no good you running off from here. How far'd you get? You're no match for them out there. You're safer in here."

Mitchie looked round, distracted, out the back door, then back at Beryl.

"I can't stay here."

"You can't go out there."

Ellie intervened. "She's right Mitchie. You have to stay here. Don't even go out the back yard."

Mitchie just stood there, her arms hanging, looking in complete despair. McCabe was still burbling in the back, "But she was fucking Maisie! How can two girls .. ?"

Flossie took him out to the saloon.

Ellie put both her hands up to her forehead.

"Jesus, Mary and Joseph! What are we gonna do? She's right, she can't stay here. How we gonna get her out?"

Beryl was thinking.

"There's a stage going tomorrow morning. Maybe we can disguise her, get her on it?"

"Disguise her? As what? A girl?"

Beryl nodded distractedly, but her mind was working. "All we have to do is hide her till we can get her out. Alright, what about McCabe's Indian friends? They could ride her out"

"She'll never pass as an Indian, her hair's too short."

"That doesn't matter. They have horses. They can get her out."

They both looked at Mitchie. Ellie nodded.

"I can't think of anything else. Where's McCabe gone now?" Ellie went off to talk to him and Mitchie looked at Beryl, eyes huge in her pale face. Beryl squeezed her shoulder.

"We'll get you out of here, down to Fort Macleod. I won't leave you, Mitchie. If you go, I'm going too."

Mitchie's eyes went even bigger as she took this in.

But down in the settlement the story ran like wildfire. The boys ran into their homes full of it, blurting it all out with shining eyes, urgent with import. The adults took it in with varying degrees of shock, disbelief, outrage, glee. They talked among themselves, went up to the General Store and hung around, chewing it over.

"That Mitchie boy? From up the whorehouse? Who'd 'a thought it?"

"Fooled me! I never would 'a guessed."

"All that time and he's a goddam girl! Well I'll be...!"

"Hey, Jungers! He came in with you, didn't he? Or she .. or whatever 'it' is. Didn't you never notice nothing?"

"Hey, Adams! You heard the latest?" and so on.

Until someone remembered about Maisie.

"Hey, wasn't he sweet on that fat girl up there? The one who died – Maisie. Hell! We saw him kissing her and fooling around. If he's a she, Maisie was fooling around with a girl!"

"Hell! She must 'a knowed if she was foolin' with 'im."

"Goddam! I'd 'a liked to see that, two girls like that, haw haw!!"

"No, that ain't natural. What're you talking about here? Two ladies, together? Like that? No – no -no no that's just plain wrong!"

One of the men who'd come in with a wife and family spoke out.

"I don't hold with having a whorehouse in a decent town, but I can see as there might be a need, you fellows not having any regular women, an' all, but two ladies don't have no business going about like man and wife. Why, where'd we all be if that kind of thing went on all over?" He looked round.

"Guess none of us 'ud be here at all, haw haw haaw!" quipped one wit, "If they all did it, I mean," he added, lamely.

Art Skinner, the store keeper, had been listening to all of this, thinking. He whispered to his brother and went out. He made his way up to Rev Tranche's house. Sarah let him in and hovered around making coffee while the men spoke. She heard the story with utter bewilderment. Mitchie? A girl? But … She almost spoke, but held back. The memory of Mitchie saying "Maisie's my girl. I would have married her," came back to her. She didn't know what to make of this shocking news. She left the kitchen and went to sit on her own in the front room. Somehow she couldn't feel Mitchie was a bad person. She'd seen the love she had for Maisie, watched her tending on her as she lay dying, been touched by it. She had liked Mitchie, wanted to help him … or her ...oh dear! Her head spun. She resorted to the one thing she knew – prayer.

There was no actual law in the settlement, the nearest was Fort Macleod, which was two or three days ride away, depending on the state of the rivers. Art Skinner and Rev Tranche decided they would get a committee of the respectable men of the settlement together – not a mob, they were clear about that – they didn't want the ruffians taking over, but both of them had motive to shut down Miss Ellie's. They would use Mitchie as the ammunition to shoot McCabe and Ellie right out of the water. Art went off and an hour or so later returned with the doctor and a couple of the more influential miners, including McKinnon, the father of the boy who'd exposed Mitchie. Sarah tried to speak to Tranche.

"Husband, I pray that you will do no wrong to that unfortunate child. I'm sure ..."

Tranche put his hand up, interrupting her.

"My dear, surely you can see that we cannot allow the continued flouting of God's holy laws that takes place hourly in that house of shame? Something must be done!"

"But this is about one young … um... person, not the whole place."

"And one who is also flouting God's laws. Does it not clearly say that a woman shall not dress as a man, nor a man as a woman? They have been allowing this iniquity under their roof and encouraged even fouler depravities, if the stories are to be believed. No, no! It must cease. The time has come!"

Sarah could not disagree with him about that dreadful place. Oh! If only they could do it by showing them the error of their ways, not by unleashing hatred and anger against them! She and Tranche would never see eye-to-eye on this, and though she admired him for his courage in standing for the Lord in all his ways, she wished he held a little more of love and forgiveness in his heart.

The other men arrived, discussed for a short while and agreed they would go to Miss Ellie's and arrest Mitchie.

"I'm not sure we have the legal right to do that," demurred the doctor.

"It is a citizen's arrest, we represent the law of this place insofar as it has any, and the law of

God is every citizens' responsibility."

"They're getting pretty riled up out there," said McKinnon, "I wouldn't like to say how it'd go by evening after everyone's had a drink or two and talked themselves up."

Tranche's lips pursed at the mention of drink.

"So, we are agreed we must arrest her?"

"Aye, and then what? Are we going to get a Mountie up here? We gotta keep her under lock and key and wait for that," said the doctor.

Skinner chipped in. "I got a good lock-up storeroom out back of my place. She can go in there."

Tranche thought a moment. "Yes, we must be seen to act according to the law. A Mountie must be brought here. We'll keep her in your lock-up Mr Skinner."

"Let's go then."

And so there was no time for Mitchie to get away before they came. Tranche and the other four men strode into the saloon while a crowd of curious and excited people gathered outside. Miss Ellie confronted them, looking like the Queen of Sheba in her own kingdom, but Tranche would have none of it.

"We have come for that young .. ah .. person, Mitchie. And if you don't hand her over to us, then we can't be responsible for the actions of the citizens of this township," he thundered.

Miss Ellie looked at the grinning, leering faces that were peering through the windows and doors of the house and back at the frightened faces of her ladies.

"And what will you do with her?"

"We will place her where no-one can do anything to her until a Mountie gets here. If not... " Tranche gestured back towards the crowd, "It'll be on your own head."

Beryl listened to this with fury. Why, he was actually inciting the mob to attack them! She could see the crowds had mainly only come up here following the delegation, to see what they'd do. She went to Mitchie, who was cowering in her room. She was so furious that Mitchie quailed at her.

"They have a mob out there! They've come to arrest you."

Mitchie gasped in panic, desperation on her face. Beryl took her by the shoulders.

"Now look! You've got to be brave. They're going to wait for a Mountie from Fort Macleod. You've got to just stay calm, don't fight them, I've got a plan. There's time. I'm not going to give you up to them. I can get you out of this, just be brave, my dear!"

As she spoke, Ellie came in, followed closely by Tranche and the 'Committee'.

Beryl and Mitchie faced them, one quietly furious, the other trembling and wide-eyed. Tranche glared in self-righteous contempt at both of them. There he was! The inescapable nightmare that had haunted Mitchie's young life, even the vastness of the Canadian West was not enough to keep him from following her, capturing her, silencing her. Tranche still did not recognize her, but to Mitchie's eyes his unflinching expression meant he was still sure he could get away with it – get away with anything. There was no escape. There never would be. He had her back in his power and was gloating at her. Her jaw clamped. There was nothing she could say to help herself. Never had been. Beryl, too, felt this was not the moment to speak out, to say what she knew of Tranche.

McCabe returned with Thomas Cloud Horse as they led Mitchie away. McCabe ducked back when he saw them, but Cloud Horse stood and watched.

"Huh! They take that girl away?" he asked McCabe.

"Goddammit! Am I the only one who didn't know he was a girl?"

"You whites are blind. Woman who want to dress as man, be a warrior; man who want to dress as woman, stay in tipi," he shrugged, "you can't fight that."

Beryl saw them and came over.

"Thomas, I need your help."

"Too late, they got her anyway." Beryl continued.

"Not if I can help it!" she glanced at McCabe, then took Cloud Horse off to one side, talking to him quietly and urgently. He nodded and left. Ellie came up.

"You're not thinking of breaking her out, are you? That'd be crazy!"

"No, I have a better plan. Ellie, didn't Mitchie tell you how she ran away back east? Don't you know who Tranche is?"

Ellie frowned, "What are you talking about? She ran away from some asshole who was raping her ..." She tailed off and gawked at Beryl. "Jesus! Tranche?! That was him?"

Beryl nodded.

"Damn! She did say the name to me, but I forgot it .. " She spun round, her hands clasping her forehead.

"Beryl, they won't listen to a word we say! It's her word against his. Who they gonna listen to?"

Beryl nodded. "We have to play this just right," she breathed out a long breath, "and I hope Mitchie will have the courage to speak out when the time comes."

McCabe appeared from behind the outhouse. Ellie looked at him dully. "And there's another liability I got myself landed with," she thought, "Goddammit! We were doing so well!"

Whatever the outcome, she knew things would change round here. Maybe it was time to move on again, but starting up anew was hard. She walked heavily back inside, followed by McCabe. Beryl continued to stand, looking across the valley at the little chapel with its bell. She lit a cigarillo and sat on the log, thinking. Either Tranche hadn't recognized Mitchie, or he was a damn good actor. She was not going to give Mitchie up without a fight, but what was happening to her now? She considered going to see Sarah Tranche. She seemed a decent woman. But if Tranche was there too, what then?

It was getting dark. The shadows of the

mountains crept across the landscape. An elk bellowed in the forest above the settlement. Wrapping her shawl about her, Beryl walked through the darkening shadows, down to where the crowd was gathered outside Skinner's Store. The doctor was speaking.

"Calm down now! We're keeping her in back here, there's no call to go creating a ruckus now. Just wait for the Mountie to get here. Everything's got to be done legal and right. Now go home, please."

Beryl slipped round behind the store, but stopped when she saw Tranche and Skinner standing there, outside a door with a padlock on it. So, that's where she is! She hesitated, then stepped forward. There was a lantern lit on a hook and they turned as she came toward them.

"You've locked her in here?" Her calm demeanour outraged Tranche, who drew himself up to his full height.

"And by what right do you come here, woman?"

"By what right do you lock up an innocent? She's done nothing wrong."

"What would a harlot know of right and wrong?" sneered Tranche.

"Too much, *Reverend* Tranche!" she stressed his title with heavy sarcasm. "I'm telling you now, both of you," she glared at Skinner, who looked evasive – after all, he'd not been too squeamish about availing himself of her services until he fell out with McCabe, "If I hear tell that either of you, or any other of your 'Committee' touches that girl while she's here, if you so much as set foot inside there, while she's helpless like that, I'll have you." Her quiet fury intimidated even Tranche. "I know what men like you are capable of. You better watch yourselves. You aren't above the law yourselves."

No-one, least of all a woman, had ever spoken to Tranche like that. Before he could rally a reply, Mitchie's voice came from inside the shed.

"Miss Beryl, is that you?" There was a catch in

her voice. You certainly could not have mistaken her for a boy, sounding like that.

"Yes, Mitchie, it's me," Beryl called back. "You alright in there?" She saw two of Mitchie's fingers trying to poke out through the gap at the side of the door. Pushing past the men, she reached out and just managed to touch her fingers to Mitchie's through the thick door.

"I guess so," said Mitchie miserably.

"Be brave, Mitchie, we'll get you out of here. We'll get at the truth here," she glanced at Tranche, assessing his reaction. He had recovered himself and said,

"Madam, I assure you no-one will go into um 'her', except my own wife, Sarah. Do not accuse us from the cesspit of your own mind." He stopped, glowering down from his considerable height, trying to intimidate Beryl.

"You see to that, Tranche, because I'll hear if anything else happens, you understand?" She turned and left.

"Suffer not a woman to speak in the

congregation", quoted Tranche.

Skinner nodded agreement and turned away. "You better get your wife, Reverend, looks like she got a job here." He tried not to sound disappointed. He had had a few thoughts on the lines of investigating at first hand if Mitchie was a normal girl, you know, or maybe if there was some interesting differences. But she'd probably scream the place down and there were too many hangers on, watching. All with pretty much the same idea in mind, but Skinner didn't want to get into anything in any public way, not with Mounties on their way. He reminded himself his main aim was to get rid of McCabe.

And so it was that Sarah Tranche tended on Mitchie for the five days it took for a Mountie to be brought up. They'd not had to go as far as the Fort, they heard tell one was riding through the territory and found him before he had returned all the way back to base.

Sarah brought Mitchie a modest grey dress and undergarments to change into.

"You must wear these now, dear. It's not proper for you to dress as a boy."

Despite her own modesty, she stood and watched while Mitchie, reluctantly, changed into the clothes. She was so thin and small-breasted it was easy to see how she'd been able to deceive people for so long. Mitchie saw her looking, checking, confirming it was really true.

"Miss Sarah, you're a good lady. I never meant no harm. If I deceived you, it wasn't coz I meant to, it's just the way it all went." She tailed off. What was the point? This woman was wife to the one who had caused all this. She was her enemy too, no matter if she was kind and good. None of them would ever understand. She'd loved Maisie. She loved Beryl. But people like them didn't care about love. They had it all wrapped up in labelled packages and they didn't care about anything that didn't fit in those packages. She finished doing up the buttons on the dress.

"There now! You look nice Mitchie. If your hair

was longer, you'd be a pretty girl! Here, wear this cap to hide your hair."

Mitchie looked at the mob cap, it was exactly like the one she threw away when she ran off from Tranche all those years ago. She shook her head.

"I ain't wearing that. People can see I'm a girl, without me wearing one of them, either that or they're just blind."

Sarah looked at her, sighed, and put it away.

The two women stood, awkwardly, looking at each other.

"You've always been good to me, Miss Sarah. Don't think I ain't grateful for the way you always tried to help. I'd 'a liked to train as a carpenter, like you offered to help me with, but you see why I couldn't take you up on it."

Sarah could think of no answer to that, but she took both Mitchie's hands and pressed them. "I pray the Lord will show us the way out of this, my dear."

Mitchie nodded.

"I think the Lord don't listen to the likes of me," she said, but thought: *"not your Lord anyway."*

Sarah left her with a copy of the Bible and some blankets and a paillasse to sleep on.

The days passed with gossip and speculation buzzing through the settlement. The boys who had seen Mitchie were questioned avidly for details, which most of them were unable to supply after such a brief and uninformed glimpse of Mitchie's privates. Sarah, of course, kept her counsel, only confirming the truth of what the boys had claimed.

"She is a girl, a young woman, a boyish figure, but quite normal" was all she would say.

She kept her counsel on other things too, about Mitchie saying Maisie was her girl. She heard some of the ugly talk of the men – how they'd teach a girl like that a lesson, how they'd show her what she was missing, even how they'd like to watch two women doing with each other before they showed them what was really what. If they saw her listening, they'd tail off in chuckles and nudges. It sent a chill through Sarah. There was nothing godly in such talk. She disapproved of Mitchie's behaviour, God had not intended women to act like men in any manner, but still, she was afraid of where all this talk could lead if these men were ever able to act on their desires. She made sure to go in and check on Mitchie to be sure she was safe. She knew nothing of what Beryl had said to her husband and Skinner, but her own forebodings were similar. At least they were doing the right thing by calling in a proper law man.

Business boomed at Miss Ellie's. At least, the bar was doing well, from all the sight-seers and lollygaggers, but there was an edge to the conversation and fewer men were paying for the women. Some of their favourite regulars were staying away.

The only other thing that happened was that Thomas Cloud Horse reappeared, accompanied by one of Beryl's occasional customers. She spent a lot of time with him, but a great deal of it was talk, not sex.

Chapter 8

Joe Skinner and a couple of other men rode in with the Mountie. They'd told him what the trouble was as they rode with him. The Mountie wasn't even sure there was a legal case against a woman dressing as a man, but his job was to keep the peace, and that was clearly needed if what the men told him was anything to go by. They wanted a trial so they could parade Mitchie before everyone and name her as a sinner and lawbreaker, to discredit her and shame the townspeople into demanding the brothel be closed. The Skinner brothers wanted McCabe run out of town, and Tranche wanted the harlots to be sent forth from their midst. The Mountie had to make sure it was a trial, not a lynch mob.

The Mountie slept a night in the most neutral home he could find, that of the doctor, who was bitterly regretting any involvement, fearing – rightly- the possible outcome of all this.

The next day everyone went to the chapel, which they had decided was the only building suitable to be used for a trial.

They had lined up the chairs of the elders of the chapel at the business end, with Tranche's usual, much larger, seat occupied by the Mountie, who looked incongruous in his red jacket amongst the black and grey and brown of the other folk. Tranche sat smugly, dominating even from a lesser seat, on his own territory and in his element. The rest of the Committee sat up there too, and the body of the chapel was full to bursting and overflowing outside, everyone wanting to see this spectacle.

Miss Ellie and Beryl came in, accompanied by a youngish man with a weather-beaten but intelligent face. They went to the front, but finding no seats free, and none willing to make way for them, they stood, facing the Committee on their seats.

Sarah was not there. Her feelings were too confused about all this. She did not want to be called as a witness to anything they'd accuse Mitchie of, and if she attended the proceedings, her loyalties would have to be with her husband, despite her misgivings. So, she stayed away, preferring instead to visit some of the sick, including one of the Cree, and do the Lord's work where it was clear what that work was.

Mitchie was brought in, to a murmur of reaction from those who had never seen her as a girl, dressed as one, even though she still wore her short hair defiantly uncovered. Her face was pale and shadowed. She looked desperately to Beryl when she came to the front and saw them there. Beryl nodded slightly to her, and made a small signal with her hand to stay calm.

To the Mountie, she looked frightened and fragile. He saw her short hair, but could see nothing else about her to object to, apart from a masculine way of moving. He called for quiet, banging on the arm of his seat.

"Gentlemen, and ladies, my name is Stuart

Jackson RCMP, and I have been called here to represent the law in this part of Alberta." He leaned forward in his seat and addressed Mitchie. "Are you the woman they call Mitchie?

Mitchie nodded.

"Speak up! Say 'yes' or 'no' so we can hear you."

Mitchie nodded again, then reluctantly added, "Yes."

"Please now tell the court your full name."

Mitchie looked from him to Tranche, who sat, impassive, no sign of recognition on his face. Silence, then, "Michelle Aubusson, sir, that's the name I was given, sir."

Tranche started and really looked at her for the first time. His eyes narrowed.

RCMP Jackson continued, "The people of this town claim you impersonated a man, Miss Aubusson. Is that true?"

Mitchie thought about this for a while, then said,

"I did dress in boy's clothes, sir, and I didn't

mind if people took me for a boy. I don't know that I ever told anyone I was actually a man, they just took me for one coz of the way I dressed."

"*Clever girl!*" thought Beryl, watching from the side. The audience laughed.

"Well, as far as I know there's no law saying a girl can't dress in boys' clothes," said Jackson.

Tranche frowned and said "God's law states 'woman shall not wear that which pertains to a man, neither shall a man put on a woman's garment: for all that do so are abomination to the Lord your God.' She has broken God's law!"

Jackson demurred, "Well, Reverend Tranche, God's laws and the laws of the British Empire do not entirely coincide. I know of no statute that dictates what men and women should wear."

Tranche's head was spinning. How could he have failed to recognize Mitchie before? There she was, after all this time, and she'd been here, right under his nose and he had been too blind to see her. Suddenly his mouth was dry and words failed him – *he* who had always known God would give him whatever words he needed. He sat, silent.

Art Skinner spoke out. "What about what she been doing with them women up there in that whorehouse? She was seen going about with Fat Maisie, kissing and that. What about that?" he looked over at Tranche, "Unnatural congress, ain't that what you called it, Reverend?"

Tranche looked back with glazed eyes and nodded. An excited murmur went through the crowd, this was what they had been waiting for.

Stuart Jackson looked over at Mitchie. "Miss Aubusson, you have a special friend, this Maisie, you are close with her?"

Mitchie got this - it was a game again, like the one she used to play when she was a boy looking for odd jobs. When she'd look very young and kind of helpless, brave but a bit desperate. That always won them round. She gave him a hurt look, kind of big-eyed, but not too cute, not here.

"Yes sir, me and Maisie were friends. She was the first girl I ever was friends with, sir, coz I always worked with men before, sir." A pause, "but she died." Mitchie looked down, she wasn't pretending now, her lip wobbled on its own, not because she was putting it on.

Skinner cut in. "She was seen kissing and carrying on like they was sweethearts!"

Mitchie shot him a look. "Course I kissed her! She was my friend. She knowed I was a girl right away, she weren't blind like everyone else."

Jackson was baffled. How did you work this one out?

"You shared a bed?"

Mitchie nodded, "Sure. They all knew I was a girl. I just like to dress in pants and stuff. There weren't no reason to put me in a separate bed. We shared that room."

"*Good girl!*" breathed Beryl. She glanced at the man next to her.

Jackson continued. "Well, did anyone actually see Miss Aubusson having … erm … unlawful congress with the other lady?"

Skinner looked furious, and turned to Tranche. Why wasn't he doing this? He always knew what to say, how to turn things his way. But Tranche sat silent and seemed lost in thought.

"Well, not exactly 'congress', sir, more … they was holding hands and … "he stopped, realizing how lame it sounded. There had only ever been rumours and occasional sightings of the pair.

"Old Hank Dowden said he saw 'em kissing each other on the mouth and they was at it for a long time, out in the trees up there. He was watching 'em for thirty minutes or so."

"I bet he was!" thought Beryl, "Enjoying every minute too!"

Mitchie was shocked to hear this. She remembered that time with Maisie. She'd so wanted to take her, out there in the woods, but Maisie didn't want to lie down on the rough forest floor, and Mitchie remembered Miss

Ellie's warning, so they went back to the house and did it there instead. She shivered at the thought of how close she'd been. When you're in love you think nothing will harm you, nothing can go wrong. She flicked a glance at Beryl, and licked her bottom lip, her mouth dry.

"So, where is this Hank Dowden, then?" asked Jackson. There was a general murmur around the chapel and Skinner admitted,

"He ain't here no more."

He shifted uncomfortably. "But we all know that's what she was doing. Her and all the carry-on up at that place." He glared belligerently at Ellie and Beryl.

The man who was with them had been watching the proceedings intently, now he stepped forward.

"Sir, I'd like to ask Miss Aubusson a few questions, if I may."

"And who might you be?" from Jackson.

"My name's Lionel Percy, sir. I'm a journalist and writer. I travel round these parts and write articles about the life out here, for the people back East. Perhaps you've read some of my articles?"

Jackson nodded. "You wrote that thing about the bald eagle, 'A Mountain Life'?"

"The very one, sir."

"But what is your interest here? This is not a side-show for you to entertain the folks back East."

"I was asked to come here, sir, by some of Miss Aubusson's friends. I trained in Law, sir, before I turned to writing. They were concerned that someone be here to represent her."

Jackson considered this, then nodded.

"I can't see there is much to defend here, but go ahead."

Percy stepped forwards, facing Mitchie.

"Miss Aubusson, can you tell us, here, when you first started to dress like a boy?"

Mitchie's eyes slid past him to Beryl, who gave a slight nod.

"It was when I ran away, sir. I didn't want men coming at me. I figured they'd leave me alone if I was a boy."

"You ran away? Where from?"

"Back East, sir, where I was before I came out here."

"But .. your family? Did you run away from your parents?"

"No, sir, I didn't have no family, not since my momma died when I was eleven."

"Ah! An orphanage then?"

Mitchie shook her head. "No, sir, I was a servant, in … someone's … house. My Momma and I were there, then she died and I was kept on."

Suddenly Tranche roused himself. "I fail to see the purpose of these questions!" he blustered.

"I can see no objection to them. I think we all need to hear a little more of Miss Aubusson's side of things," Jackson replied firmly.

"So, then, 'Mitchie', that is the name you prefer?" Percy smiled at her. She nodded.

"So, Mitchie, you ran away from the place where you were a servant? Did they ill-treat you?"

Mitchie hesitated. She'd been five nights with almost no sleep, terrified and alone. Now she was here, things didn't seem so bad. That Mountie was taking the wind out of Tranche and Skinner, but she felt the hostility of the folk around her. And now this man wanted to know why she ran away. Suddenly she was shaking, visibly. She fought with herself, finally she just nodded.

Jackson leaned forward, "Speak up, Miss Aubusson."

Shakily Mitchie spoke. "Yes sir, he ill-treated me."

"He?'He' ill-treated you? Were you beaten? Was your mistress unkind?"

The occasional beating and harsh words were quite acceptable in the treatment of servants, not, by any means, an excuse to run away.

Mitchie's head was spinning. "No, sir, I didn't

have no mistress, only a master." Involuntarily, she glanced over at where Tranche was sitting.

All this was so unexpected for Tranche. Things always went his way, his dominating presence usually overpowered people, mesmerized them. Now it was all slipping away! He felt faint, he was sweating. He took out a large handkerchief and dabbed his forehead and his mouth. Nausea welled up in his belly.

Percy spoke very gently to Mitchie, but his voice was clear to the rapt gathering.

"I think you need to tell us what happened, Mitchie."

Mitchie's face broke and she began to sob. She looked like a little girl, an eleven year old in a seventeen year old body.

"I can't say! Don't ask me to! I ain't allowed to say! He'll kill me if I do!"

Apart from her sobbing, you could hear a pin drop. What further delicious depravity was going to thrill the folk now? Beryl stepped to Mitchie's side and put her arm round her.

"Sh-h-sh, Mitchie, it's alright. You *can* tell now." She shot a glance at Jackson.

"Miss Aubusson, I think you *do* need to tell us. Don't be afraid."

"He.. he used to come at me. In the nights."

"What do you mean, 'come at' you?"

Mitchie's face was streaming tears. "You know, with his thing, b ..between his legs. He'd stick it in me. In there .." and she pointed to her crotch.

"How can she manage to sound so naïve after two years in a brothel?" Beryl wondered, *"But, well done, my love!"* and she gently squeezed Mitchie's shoulder.

There were gasps from the townspeople. Most of them weren't sure whether to be thrilled or disgusted.

Percy waited for them to quieten, then

"Mitchie, I need to ask you a couple more things. Do you think you can carry on?"

Mitchie stared numbly at him, snot running down her face, then she nodded.

"How old were you when you ran away?"

"Thirteen, sir."

"I see. And how long had your master been 'coming at' you before you ran away?"

"Since I was eleven, sir. After my Momma died. He came at her too. That's why she died. She bled to death, from there," and again she pointed at her crotch. Percy had not been expecting her to say that, but it was right on target.

"So, you are telling me you and your mother lived with this 'gentleman' as his servants, and he had relations with your mother, until she died, then he started with you?"

Mitchie stared out of her tears.

"He weren't no relation of ours. He just took us in."

A ripple of amusement ran through the room, but most were listening avidly. Some were even feeling sorry for this waifish young woman.

"I mean 'came at' you. Mitchie."

Mitchie bowed her head, nodding dumbly.

"And your mother haemorrhaged to death." Percy sighed loudly and shook his head.

"Mitchie, just one more question. Who was your master? What was his name?"

Mitchie looked desperately at him, her face crumpling. She glanced over at Jackson, at Tranche, and back at Percy.

"Don't ask me that! I can't say!"

"Why are you still so afraid, Mitchie? This all happened back east, what is there to be afraid of here?"

Mitchie was incoherent. She fought to speak, but it seemed all her senses were filled with the dark presence of Tranche, his smell overwhelmed her, gagged her and her body was seized and tiny in his grasp, as it had been before. The gathered people watched her agonized expression as she swayed and looked ready to faint.

"Mitchie, are you afraid because the man who did that to you is not far away back East? Is perhaps nearby, even *in here* now?"

Mitchie nodded.

"Speak up, Miss Aubusson." commanded Jackson. "The man is here, you say?"

"Yes sir."

"Then you must tell us. Point to him, Miss Aubusson."

Everyone was looking round, agog with curiosity.

Percy urged her, "Come now, Mitchie, point to him. Can you see him from here?"

Beryl held her tightly round the shoulder and kept herself from looking over at Tranche.

Mitchie turned herself slightly to her right and raised her arm, pointing to the row of elders' chairs, then she looked directly into the face of her tormentor and abuser and said

"That's him! Mr Tranche, Reverend Matthew Tranche, he was my master. He done that to me!"

The building erupted in shouting. Cries of "No!

This can't be true," and "You hear that? She said Tranche!" and the like burst out from all sides.

Tranche sat like a stone, still towering over them, seated as he was. He held Mitchie in a long gaze, while Jackson shouted above the hubbub and banged his heel on the wooden plank flooring, for quiet.

Tranche stood up and finally everyone quietened.

"Outrageous! Pure lies! I've never seen this girl before I came here. How can this be true? She's lived here for nearly two years, befriended by my wife, seeing me- she stood right by me when I buried her friend Maisie, and she never said a word about this. I was as close to her then as I am now, and that was the first time I had ever set eyes upon her." He glared round the room, at *his* congregation. "It's obvious she has been put up to this. Look at the way that … harlot... is prompting her, urging her to speak the words they have put in her mouth." Beryl suddenly realized how it looked with her standing by Mitchie, helping her.

"Oh, yes! What a clever plan! Her and you, Mistress Ellie, both of you sunk in your pit of sin, using this poor child to attack the one who daily preaches against everything you stand for."

He was back! In control. As always. His arrogant self-belief never failed him, God was on *his* side and righteousness *would* prevail.

Mitchie cringed back as Tranche seemed to grow before her eyes. She put her hands up as if warding off something.

"No, no! Please don't let him...!" she whispered.

Percy faced Tranche calmly.

"Presumably some of this can be verified, sir. There will be records in your former congregation of whether you had a servant called Michelle Aubusson. It's a rather uncommon name. We can track down the truth of this."

Jackson cut in.

"Mr Percy, this matter cannot be pursued further here. Miss Aubusson has made an accusation that cannot be substantiated."

Suddenly Mitchie darted forward and seized the large Bible that was kept open on a stand at the front, it was heavy but she picked it up and held it out in front of her.

"I swear, I swear on this Bible, that I was telling the truth." She remembered some words she had read in one of Beryl's books. "It was the truth, the whole truth, and nuthin but the truth, so help me God!"

The corners of Tranche's mouth pulled down and his eyebrows seemed to bristle as he stared back at Mitchie, "She lies! Look at them, urging her on!" he thundered, in his best pulpit voice.

"Quiet!" roared Jackson. The room subsided again.

"Miss Aubusson, return the Bible to its stand."

Mitchie almost dropped it, but Percy took it

from her.

"Miss Aubusson, I am releasing you. I can find no crime you have committed. And I demand assurances that you will not be molested any further by the citizens of this settlement." Jackson looked out over the assembled townsfolk, and then back at Mitchie. "I can only advise you, in future, to dress and behave in a manner appropriate to your sex."

He paused. "As for this other matter, you have made a serious accusation, but at present there is no case against the man you have accused. We cannot pursue it any further here. I declare these proceedings closed and you are free to leave – all of you." He glared again at the chattering people.

Mitchie looked bewildered for a moment, then bowed her head. She turned to Beryl who was white-faced and furious. She and Tranche exchanged a poisonous look. Jackson beckoned Percy over to talk to him further about his writings. Mitchie, Beryl and Ellie stood together, unable to leave for the crush of people, but Tranche turned and walked out the small door at the end of the chapel, the one he normally used for services. Skinner followed him, but the doctor wanted nothing more to do with them, so he filed out with the rest of the people.

Finally they were able to return to the house with Mitchie. They walked into the kitchen, where most of the rest of the women were. She was so emotionally drained, she could barely stand. Ellie and Beryl had had to hold on to her, each to an arm, to get her up the hill. Lionel Percy followed them, looking thoughtful.

Beryl took Mitchie straight to her room while Ellie fielded the questions of the others. Beryl closed the door then held Mitchie tight.

"You did so well! You were so brave, my dear," she whispered into Mitchie's hair. Then she took Mitchie's face in her hands and said, "I love you, Michelle Aubusson," and smiled at her.

Mitchie's throat was clogged. She whispered, "I don't know why I feel so bad!"

"Oh baby! You're exhausted. And that bastard still got away with it … but you did right, you told the truth and that's what matters."

Mitchie nodded and sat on the bed, legs apart, boy-fashion in her grey skirt. Beryl knelt in front of her, concerned.

"I'll get you a hot drink, baby – maybe put some drops in. You'll feel better after you've had a chance to get some sleep."

Mitchie put her arms round Beryl's neck, saying nothing, just smelling the scent of her hair and feeling the warmth of her.

Beryl whispered, "You're with me now, you're alright." She rose, "I'll be right back."

Mitchie nodded.

She looked down at the clothes she was wearing, worked the boots off her feet – they had left her those anyway. She began to unbutton the top, but then, just lay down on her side. When Beryl returned with hot milk and a bottle of laudanum, Mitchie was already asleep. She pulled the quilt up over her, stood and looked down at her for a long moment, then went out and shut the door.

Percy was standing in the kitchen, drinking coffee and listening to the women chat about Mitchie. None of them were especially surprised to find out a Minister had taken advantage of Mitchie when she was just a child – nor were they surprised Mitchie and Percy's exposure of him had come to nothing. It only confirmed what most of them already expected from respectable society. They shrugged it away.

"Mitchie looks strange in a dress," giggled Flossie, "She still walks like a boy."

"Yeah, like she got a melon between her legs!" Laughter.

"They ain't none of 'em got anything that big between their legs!"

Beryl came from Mitchie's room and took Percy's hand, smiling at him.

"You coming?" she said softly to him. He nodded and they both went up to her room.

Beryl lit up a cigarillo and offered one to him. They sat side by side on the bed and put their feet up, kicking off their shoes.

"I guess that went as well as could be expected," she said, trying not to sound too disappointed.

"Hmm, at least Mitchie's free and I will see what I can dig up. I have a friend back there, on the Times, who will look into what he can get on him."

Beryl nodded. "Thank you Lionel for this, I owe you."

He chuckled, "You know, Beryl, I'd marry you if I thought you'd take me."

She looked at him, astonished.

"Why not?" he said, "you're an educated, cultured woman, beautiful too. You're too damn good for place like this. We'd suit each other."

"Oh, Lionel, if I was ever going to be the marrying kind, I'd take you, but …. "she shook her head. They grinned ruefully at each other.

"So, will you and Mitchie leave here, you

think?" he asked.

"I haven't even thought about that," replied Beryl. But she was wondering where all this would lead. There was an edge to the loud voices of the men who trooped in to the saloon. Beryl wasn't intending to go down and work tonight. She turned back to Lionel.

"You want to …?" she grinned. He smiled back, considering, then nodded.

"It may be my last chance," he said and leant over to kiss her. She kissed him back, then began to unbutton her blouse.

Chapter 9

Reverend Tranche strode grimly past the curious onlookers when he left the chapel. Art Skinner panted by his side, hard put to keep up with Tranche's long legs. He darted curious looks at Tranche's face, assessing. He'd allied himself with him in a common aim, to get rid of McCabe and Miss Ellie's establishment, but Skinner couldn't stand the man.

"Anyone that self-righteous probably does have something to hide," he thought. "If it's true he's already had that Mitchie girl then the whorehouse was probably the best place for her.

Hmm! Maybe we'll all get a chance at her now, now we know she ain't no pure as snow virgin like she been making out."

Tranche stopped walking, bringing Skinner's thoughts to a halt.

"I bid you good day, Art Skinner," he said, touching his hat. Then he turned and marched up to his house.

Skinner's almost black eyes narrowed in his fleshy face as he watched him go.

"Good day to you, too," he muttered and turned back for home.

When Tranche got into his house there was no sign of his wife, Sarah. The house was deserted, even the housekeeper was out. He sat by the table, his jaw rigid around clenched teeth. His Bible lay open on the table and his hand went to it by habit, but he did not pull it to him and read. Mitchie fluttered through his thoughts, the image of her in the grey, demure dress blending with that younger one of her in a nearly identical brown one. How had someone he had discarded from his life for so long, been able to come back and act in such a way? Even now, he saw Mitchie as no more than a tool, being used by others. After all, what else had she ever been?

His fury focussed on the two harlots who had accompanied her, and brought in their paid monkey to speak for them. They had been clever, oh yes! Priming her before they'd been able to remove Mitchie from their clutches. He wondered if the journalist would try to find out anything from his old congregation. Pah! Small matter if they did. It was still only Mitchie's word against his.

His thoughts drifted back to the day Mitchie had vanished. He was angry when he came home to find the house cold and dark, no food ready for him. Only gradually did he realize she was nowhere in the place. Then the members of his congregation had rallied round, sending out messages to the authorities to search for her. He'd gone up to her room in the attic to look around, and there he'd found the picture of her mother under her pillow. That whore! All that talk about her dead husband! He'd been assured she was a respectable widow, but she'd never said a word when he started to come to her in bed, never cried out or protested. Oh no! She'd waited until she was pregnant then started complaining. As if he would marry such a one!

Her daughter was just the same after her. The

Bible clearly states that if a woman does not cry out and she is in a town or near others who can hear her, when a man takes her by force, then it was she who was to blame and it was not deemed to be rape. And Mitchie had waited until now, when she clearly had something to gain from it, then suddenly decided to cry out and protest, when she'd lain there all those times, opening her legs like any common little street whore. Small wonder she'd ended up in a whorehouse, she wasn't fit for anything better.

His congregation had made sure the next woman they sent to him as housekeeper was built like a bulldog and over fifty, but that did not mean they suspected him of anything. Much less that they would speak out against him if Lionel Percy came asking. He'd soon made sure to find himself a young, pretty wife after that. It was better like that, less chance of misguided gossip. He had come out here to a new place that was clean and pure, unpolluted by the temptations of a city. And his wife, too, was chaste and pure, worthy of him; when she lay with him, it was with seemly modesty, quietly, as a dutiful wife should, not wriggling and squirming under him, inciting his lust like that little ..... He stopped those thoughts.

Now it was the other two his thoughts landed on. Mitchie was terrified, and so inconsequential. But a woman who is proud and defies a man, is an abomination. And those two were both proud. They were incapable of modesty, even in a holy building and a court of law.

Rising, he went upstairs and lay on the bed, staring at the ceiling. After a while he got up and went to his drawer, to a leather case inside the drawer. He opened it and pulled aside the papers and old photographs in it, uncovering a small, framed picture of a woman's face. His mouth pulled down as he looked at it, he turned it over to read the name on the back – 'Rachel Aubusson'. With a violent movement he threw it on the floor and stamped on it, hard and repeatedly, till the cheap frame had come apart and a tear appeared on one corner of the picture inside. He stood for a long while, leaning on the chest of drawers, staring at himself in the mirror on top of it. Then he turned and went out, and out of the house. He walked down to find the McKinnon boy and his friends.

Sarah Tranche walked back to the settlement as the shadows lengthened in the early mountain dusk. Her visit to the Cree camp has taken longer than planned, somehow she'd found it impossible to withstand the requests for help from this one and that. And sitting with them, their women, talking in the long, slow way of those people - their silences between each response used to make her uncomfortable, but today she'd found it oddly restful. She'd sat for far too long in their quietness, watching the most beautiful bead-work emerge from the fingers of one skilled ancient, listening to the odd sounds of their language when they spoke to each other, though their English was adequate. And then she'd returned to reality, remembered today was the trial of Mitchie, realized guiltily she had deserted her husband when the dear man was doing his best to stand for righteousness and his Lord.

She knew that whatever had been decided was long over now. She was confident that no harm would come to Mitchie, surely all they would do was reprove her and order her to mend her ways, to dress properly. And as for the stories about her and poor Maisie, what point was there in bringing that up? Maisie was dead anyway, and Mitchie was so young, it was natural for her to develop a crush on her dear friend, and maybe to imagine it was more than it was. Perhaps Matthew would agree to take Mitchie in, to work for them, to help her back into society.

But she had not been there for dear Matthew. She sighed. She knew he was a good man, but sometimes he was a little too much the man, the warrior fighting for the word of God in a world of iniquity. She could never persuade him to be a little less unbending, a little less … well

.. harsh in his judgements. But he was right really. She was just a weak woman, using charm and persuasion, while he was brave and steadfast in bearing witness to the Living God.

As she walked along the ridge leading to the valley of the settlement, the sounds her own people rose up, magnified in the cooling, moist air. A clang of machinery, the bark of a dog, and there, a waft of music and laughter. She looked across the valley and saw Miss Ellie's establishment, a soft glow of light came through its open doors. There seemed to be more people than usual up there. Another strain of music drifted up to her again.

She looked over at the chapel, not far below her. It was dark and quiet. Sunday seemed a long way off. Oh dear! Poor Matthew! He'd had such hopes for today. She knew he had nothing against Mitchie, it was only his desire to make the people see what a terrible place that was, to get them to see the error of allowing it to carry on like that. And now he'd be so disappointed.

Her gaze travelled to their own house. It too was dark. Well, Violet, their housekeeper, would be in the kitchen at the back, it was not yet quite dark enough to light the lantern, the band of darkness from the mountain had not yet reached their side of the valley.

Suddenly Sarah felt guilty. Her hours in the Cree camp now felt like a little holiday, far from all the cares and work of home, and now her neglected duties crowded in on her. She made her way to the chapel and let herself in by the side door.

The reddish light shone through the west windows, showing her the seats of the elders arranged slightly differently than normal. There was a stuffy smell, the residue of many bodies crowded in and breathing each other's air. The Bible on its stand was crooked. She straightened it, then opened it at random, as she often did. It opened at the little Book of Ruth. She went and sat on the front pew, where she should have been sitting earlier today - as always in services, eyes on her husband, at his side, a helpmeet and support.

She began to pray, sending out a silent call to God. "Show me my duty, Lord! Those women, they can't see that they besmirch the image of God in themselves, when they sell themselves. The men too! Why does no-one speak of the shame of the men, who even more are made in the image of God, only to drag it in the dirt when they abuse themselves with harlots? If only they could be made to see."

A shaft of light fell on the Bible on the stand. It was facing away from her, she could only see the back of the simple wooden stand, but she knew the pages it had opened at. Her mind seized the image of Ruth, patient mother of Jesse, the root that had produced the branch from which Jesus himself was descended. All those centuries before, she had patiently sat amongst the harlots at the gate of the City, refusing to give in until she was treated with honour and her son was recognized by his father's family. If not for her, the branch that produced Jesus would never have existed. Oh yes! It was a sign! The Lord had spoken to her. She would go and sit patiently, stubbornly amongst the harlots until all of them, the men and those women, could see what they were really doing, could see, as she, Sarah, saw, that each of them could be a temple to God if only they would stop what they were doing and turn to the Lord.

She stood up, took a deep breath and squared her shoulders. Then she marched out of the chapel. As she closed the door behind her, the heavy Bible slid off the stand and hit the floor with a loud thud. It lay there, its cover bent and split, one page torn on the corner. Oblivious to this, Sarah marched across to the track up to the brothel, head held up and a determined glint in her eyes.

When she got there, she hesitated a moment outside, heart pounding, but this was her moment to be a soldier for Christ, to show Matthew that she was still his helpmeet. The door opened and a gust of music and laughter burst out. A man swayed down the steps, hitching up his pants and grinning. He glanced at her, past her, then he was gone. Sarah stepped up to the door and pushed in.

The smell of warm bodies, tobacco, beer and whiskey hit her unaccustomed nostrils. A man was sitting at a piano to the left of the door and there was a bar along the left wall. She focussed her gaze on McCabe as she stepped forward into the centre of the room. The carpet under her feet was reasonably clean and more luxurious than anything they had at home. There were women dressed in a most extraordinary way, sitting with men along the walls, on soft chairs and chesterfields; men standing at the bar; and Miss Ellie, facing her from the far side. Sarah's eyes travelled up to a gallery above with doors leading off, and behind Ellie she could see the door that she presumed led into the back room and kitchen where she had come to see Maisie that time.

Miss Ellie came towards her, her face hostile.

"What the hell are you doing here? What do you want?" she demanded. She vaguely recalled noticing Sarah hadn't been in the court that morning.

"I come here to speak not of Hell, Miss Ellie,

but of Heaven!"

Ellie tutted and rolled her eyes.

"Save your prayers for yourself, you're gonna need them!"

A small frown appeared for a moment on Sarah's face, then cleared.

"I was not at court this morning. Where is Mitchie now?"

Ellie's mouth pulled down at the corners.

"She's here, getting over what your lot put her through," she retorted.

"Oh but surely she should not have returned here. We would have cared for her, helped her."

Ellie's eyebrows rose. She realized Sarah had no idea what had happened. Goddammit! What did the stupid woman want here?

"Miss Sarah, you are not welcome here. You do not belong here – whatever you think you are doing – just go!" She saw Sarah's chin set and her eyes widen in defiance.

"I will stay! I have come to bear witness to the Lord," her voice rose, "I will stand here until I have shamed every one of you into leaving." She glared round at the roomful of people, trying to meet their eyes, but they glanced away, even as they were watching avidly to see what she would do.

"You should be ashamed of yourselves! Can't you see that you demean yourselves when you demean these poor women?"

Ellie's mouth dropped open. "Are you crazy? Get out of here, Sarah. You don't have any idea what you are doing!"

"I will stay here, Mistress Ellie, unless you remove me with force."

Miss Ellie fought the urge to punch Sarah right on the nose. But then a snigger from Roxie, over on the chesterfield, cut though the silence. The man on whose knee she sat joined in, his hands circling Roxie's waist and ostentatiously curling up to her breast. A few more chuckles came from other parts of the saloon. Beryl came out of her room and leant her elbows on the rail of the gallery to see what was going on. Ellie sneered at Sarah.

"Suit yourself!" she said, "Stay there! Much good it may do you!" and stamped over to the bar. She signalled to the piano player to carry on. A few men did leave, shamefacedly gulping down their drinks and donning their hats as they scurried out the door. Sarah took hold of an empty chair, sat on it and taking out her pocket Bible, began to read it out loud. The Sermon on the Mount. Her voice was shaking but she carried on. The music and laughter drowned her out.

Over at the bar, McCabe laughed to Ellie, "She's not bad-looking, you know. You should offer her a job."

"Hmph!" growled Ellie, "her face'd sour milk. Goddammit! I hate religious people!" she poured herself a large straight whiskey and glared at Sarah. Beryl appeared, cat-like, at Ellie's side, with Lionel Percy in tow.

"What's going on?"

"That's going on!" Ellie gestured at Sarah, sloshing her whiskey out of her glass as she did so. She poured herself more. "You working tonight, Beryl?"

Beryl shook her head, "Only with Lionel." She grinned, "I have to pay him back for his help today. We're just going to get something to eat." They both went into the back.

Ellie continued to drink. The noise of the saloon washed around her. Everything sounded normal, if you didn't look at the crazy woman sitting there, but Ellie felt a depression hovering over her.

"In a year's time I expect we'll all be out of here," she thought, and looked at McCabe. "Where will he be then?"

Beryl and Lionel Percy were in the kitchen. She made coffee and fried eggs, while he sawed at a loaf of bread.

"You think Mitchie'll want some?" he asked. Beryl looked over at the door of Mitchie's room.

There was no sign or sound of movement in there. She shook her head.

"Let her sleep. She was exhausted. I'll get her something later."

They ate and went back upstairs.

But Mitchie wasn't in her room. She'd woken suddenly out of a deep sleep, nightmares receding into broken fragments as she struggled to consciousness. What had woken her? Not the noise from the saloon, she was used to that. No! Just before she woke, she dreamed, what was it? She'd felt a touch, heard her mother's voice call her, 'Mitchie! Mitchie!' It was so real. She thought she'd really heard it. She lay quietly a while, tears trickling sideways across her face.

Then she sat up, sniffing, and wiped her eyes and nose. She needed a piss, wanted to move, didn't know what to do with herself. She put on her men's jacket and pulled on her boots, re-buttoning the dress. She went out the back door to the out-house. There was no-one else out here, though she could hear people out front talking loudly, a few cat-calls. She didn't want to see anyone, she was afraid of how men would treat her now, but she needed to move.

She went up to check on the pig. There were no chooks now, after the fox got in there and killed them all. The pig came over, snuffling. No-one had fed her, poor thing. Mitchie went and got some food and returned. The pig squealed and grunted, and hungrily snorted up the food in the mud. Mitchie fetched water too, and some more food. Then she sat down in her favourite place on the ground, with her back to a tree stump that had sprouted a whole lot of new shoots after it was cut down. The fence of the pigsty used this as a corner post, but the pig had not been able to destroy all the shoots that grew outside its little enclosure.

Mitchie could just see the edge of the chapel roof from here if she leaned a little sideways.

She was used to sitting out in the woods alone, as a boy she'd often needed to spend time away from the others – not just to piss and stuff, but to get away from all their rough-housing and back talking. And before that, she'd had to spend long hours on her own in Tranche's house. She'd got used to it, so it became a regular need.

She sat a long time, thinking. One minute everything had been so good, she had a place, a future, safety, friends, someone she loved. Now nothing felt safe or assured. She couldn't live here anymore. She could feel the fear like a little curdle in her belly. She'd tell Beryl as soon as she could she was going. Even if she got away, would Tranche follow her again? Would he somehow turn up like some goddam burr stuck on her that would never come off, no matter how she batted and swiped at it? She felt leaden at the thought of him. She knew he'd always get things to go his way. He even managed to persuade that decent, kind Sarah to marry him.

She heard movement in the woods behind her

and shrank into the undergrowth, freezing. They came closer. She pulled her feet and the hem of the dress in close, hunching down, barely breathing. They emerged on the other side of the pigsty, stopped at the back end of it. Mitchie was sure there was more than one.

"Oh my god! This is it! This is what I was scared of, them coming hunting for me, sneaking in from the back!" Her heart pounded and she still tried not to breathe.

"Here, give it ta me," she heard.

Whose voice was that? Oh! That McKinnon boy! She heard a sound of liquid pouring, muttered instructions, a catch of breath. Then more steps approaching, clumsy these, louder, stumbling over the rocky forest floor. This was someone bigger, breathing loudly. He arrived, and spoke, "You've got it?"

It was Tranche's voice.

"Yes sir," two voices replied, McKinnon and who was that other one? Mitchie didn't care, all she heard was Tranche.

"Watch carefully, now," he said, "Wait till there's no-one outside to see you. You're sure you know what you're doing with these?"

"Sure," McKinnon's voice, "Only thing is, I ain't sure we got good dry matches."

"Here, take this." Tranche.

"Hey! That's a mighty fine match box there, must be real silver!"

As they spoke, a smell wafted over to Mitchie - kerosene!

The other boy's voice spoke, "Won't they get hurt?" he sounded frightened.

"Naaaw! Just scare 'em a little. Like a stink bomb, only worse."

"You must not be afraid to stand against sin, boy," said Tranche, back on form, sure of his ground. "You'll be seen as heroes. Be brave and stand for what is righteous."

"Look, you don't have to throw 'em, just hold the matches and light 'em when I tell you. I'll throw 'em." McKinnon again.

"Can I hold it now? Is it real silver? Hey! Is that

an eagle on it?"

"You can hold it when we get there."

The voices faded as they walked off, but Mitchie knew Tranche was still nearby.

She knew what they were going to do, the kerosene, that talk of matches and throwing something. Oh my! They were going to set fire to Miss Ellie's! She had to get down there and warn them, but she could not run fast enough, not getting up from where she was hunkered down, and cramped in her legs like she was. If Tranche saw her, she had no doubt whatsoever that he would kill her to prevent her warning them. Identifying him.

"Oh please, please! Make him go," she prayed.

Carefully, slow inches at a time, she lowered herself onto her side, twisted round to look back with her face near the ground, her feet still tucked back, making herself as small as possible. There he stood, grim-faced like Death itself, or the Devil, more like. He was looking past her at the house, watching it, or the boys as they made their way down to it. Then he seemed to bring himself back, grunted, and turning made off back the way he'd come.

Mitchie waited till he was far enough off it didn't matter if he saw her, then she took off down the slope, running quietly, holding her skirt and dodging behind a bush, hoping

Tranche couldn't see her, darting past the log seat and into the kitchen.

Beryl and Lionel Percy sat upstairs on Beryl's bed again, drinking brandy from a bottle they held on the bed between them.

"I've found a place up there in the mountains that I've put in a claim for," he said, "it's the most perfect place on Earth. I'm going to build me a home and work from there, writing and studying."

Beryl smiled.

"You could come and live there with me," he looked at her earnestly, "I'd write and you'd play your music. We'd keep horses. Mitchie could come too."

Beryl laughed in her throat as she always did, and shook her head.

"It sounds wonderful Lionel, but crazy. Are you thinking you'll have two wives?"

He chuckled, "A wife and a younger brother, more like. They can put a dress on that one and she'll still be a boy."

"It couldn't work, I just want to be with Mitchie. It would be impossible, you'd want to be with me when I'd want to be with her."

He shook his head. "I'll never understand that. I mean, you don't mind this," he gestured at the two of them on the bed, "why is Mitchie so important to you?"

"I know, I enjoy sex with men well enough, and I like you a lot, but it's not the same. It's not what I really want." She sipped slowly at her brandy. "If I didn't have Mitchie, I'd still be wishing for someone like her. I've always been that way." She kissed him, "I could never marry you, but thank you anyway. You're the best man I've ever known."

"But you'll have to leave here. Mitchie will have to," Lionel said.

Beryl nodded, "Yes, it's time I got out of this business."

"What will you do? How will you live?"

Beryl looked smug.

"Because, my dear, I have done what most whores only talk about doing. I have saved everything I could over the years. I've got enough now to stop working. I only came to this God-forsaken place because there's good earnings and absolutely nothing to spend it on. And," she added, "I don't have everything in a sock under my mattress. It's all invested. I've been playing the stock market for years." She grinned at him. "If I did go and live with you, I'd probably be supporting you."

He chuckled.

"I suppose I shouldn't be surprised, Beryl, you're a remarkable – and intelligent - woman." He looked longingly at her. "Just the woman for me." He shook his head ruefully. "You have enough to live on?"

"Enough to invest in a business."

"A brothel?"

"Oh no!" She looked off into the distance of her imagination, "No, a shop, back East. Montreal maybe. Selling music and musical instruments. After all, I know all about it from my father. And there's plenty who remember his name. I can trade on that, if they don't just remember him drunk, that is."

He frowned. "Aren't there plenty who'd remember you too, back there? For a different reason? Why don't you settle out West? Vancouver is quite the coming place now, they say."

Beryl inclined her head, "Maybe. That's not a bad idea. Is there anyone in Vancouver who'd know what musical instruments are for?"

Percy grinned and put on a hokey accent, "When they stop wrastling grizzly baaars and take the plug o' baccy outta they mouths I hear they even speak normal English!" They laughed together.

Suddenly, from below they heard a crash of broken glass and screams and shouts, then another terrible scream. They both jumped from the bed and ran out the door to see what was going on. It was pandemonium.

Flames licked up from the centre of the room, people were running and jumping all around, diving out the door and struggling with each other. And there, right where she'd been sitting all this time with her Bible, was Sarah Tranche, screaming and screaming while the flames licked up her and around her.

To give him credit, McCabe tried to get to her, but the kerosene had splashed all over the carpet, soaking it and setting it alight. No-one could get to her. Lionel ran down the stairs and tried from his side, but the flames were already bursting out from the inflammable carpet, fanned by the open doors front and back, funnelling up. Sarah was silent now, only a dark shape in the centre of the flames, still upright for a ghastly moment, before falling over. Beryl grabbed Lionel and ran back into her room, across it, yanking the window open, climbing out on to the roof of the back room. Other windows were open and women and clients were picking their way across the roof, hanging from the other side, being helped down. Smoke billowed from the open windows. Beryl heard Mitchie's voice shrill and screaming. She got herself down and ran to her.

"He killed his own wife! That good lady, he killed her!" She was sobbing, hysterical.

Beryl looked round and saw Ellie, who was distraught; McCabe holding his burnt hands. She looked back at Mitchie. "What do you mean? Who did this?"

"Tranche! It was Tranche. He told them boys to do it! But it was him. He gave them his matchbox." Her voice was shrill, hoarse with smoke.

Beryl looked back at the burning building. Tranche did this!

Others were listening to what Mitchie was still saying, her voice hoarse from repeating it, pleading to be heard. And the two boys were brought over, they had been caught immediately. The younger one blubbered, and pleaded, he didn't ever mean to cause any harm. But they both confirmed Tranche had put them up to it.

The mob turned and ran toward the chapel and the house up behind it.

Beryl put her arms round Mitchie's shoulders, pulled her close, and held her.

"You're coming with me, my love," she shouted into her ear, over the sounds of the flames taking down Miss Ellie's establishment.

Lionel Percy looked at the woman he had come to love and respect. She had no eyes for him at all.

He walked away.